CAIN
The Seventh Day Series Book Four
By Leslie Swartz

Copyright 2020, Leslie Swartz

Library of Congress Control Number: 2020909997

ISBN: 9798649425551

He who has a why to live can bear almost any how.

Friedrich Nietzche

Prologue

"I will call her Thaddea because she is my heart," Allydia said, her voice barely above a whisper as the light in her eyes began to fade. She looked down at her newest daughter and smiled.

"You are pale," Lilith fussed. "There is too much blood. Your father will not forgive me if I let you die."

"But I *am* dying. There is nothing you can do. He will understand."

"He will leave me."

"Perhaps he can ask his God, this Elohim he claims to worship, to save me," she smirked.

"I wouldn't mock such things if I were you, girl."

"Tell Farhan I am sorry. I failed to give him a son...again. You will help him, won't you? Help care for my daughters?"

"I will not have to," Lilith insisted.

"I can feel death's grip tight around my throat. The dark fog of him shrouds the room. I am leaving this world."

"You are not." But as she said the words, her step-daughter's eyes rolled back and closed. Her chest, once heaving as she labored to breathe, fell and went still. She was gone.

Lilith gathered the baby in her arms, left the birthing tent, and presented her husband with his grandchild.

"A girl," she told him. "To be called Thaddea."

Cain took the infant, gave her an approving nod, and handed her back.

"Forgive me, husband, but your daughter..."

"My daughter what?" he snapped.

She took a step back. "She is gone."

Cain's eyes flashed and his jaw tightened. He turned toward his son-in-law sleeping next to the fire and pounced. He pulled him up by the hair and began punching him. The startled man backed away and put his hand to his jaw, the look of confusion on his face driving Cain further into madness.

"You knew this would happen!" he spat. "You knew a woman in her thirty-first year can not withstand childbirth, yet you insisted. You forced her to endure this *again* because *you wanted a son*. Now, you still have no son and I have no daughter. *You took her from me* and I will make you suffer for it." He grasped Farhan's throat and squeezed until his hand cramped. His heart pounded in his ears as he allowed the rage to overtake him. The man tried to fight back, but as he struggled, he caught a glimpse inside the tent where his wife's body lay. As his heart broke, he accepted his punishment, the thought of living without her too much to bear.

Cain pulled a knife from his belt. "I will ensure you never get what you want." With three quick strokes, he cut through the man's genitals, mutilating them beyond use and causing him to bleed out. "I only wish your death to be slower and more painful than hers." He dropped Farhan to the sandy ground and kicked him in the ribs before entering the tent. There, he saw his daughter, ashen and lifeless, and fell to his knees.

"My sons have all left me," he sobbed as Lilith followed him inside. "She followed me here to Eridu so I wouldn't be alone. She gave me grandchildren. She befriended you the moment I announced our marriage. She was kind, even when I showed her no mercy. She is the only one of my children that doesn't despise me. She deserves better than this." He looked up at his wife, tears streaming down his face. "Is this another one of His punishments? Banishing me from my home, compelling me to wander, never able to settle...is that not enough? Does He hate me this much?"

"It's unlikely my Father has thought of you in years." She placed the baby again in his arms. "He tends to put a plan in motion and move on, having His minions do His work for Him." She knelt next to him and put a comforting hand on his shoulder. "I could bring her back if you like."

"With your magic?" he sneered, rocking the quiet baby as she slept.

"Yes. Powerful blood magic. It would have to be done quickly, before her soul reaches Heaven."

"Are you serious?"

"Deadly. But," she pushed the blanket away from Thaddea's face. "It would require a sacrifice."

Cain's expression turned dark as he realized what she was getting at. "Farhan is near death already. *He* will--"

"It must be a blood relative."

"Then take my life. It's not as though I won't return."

"That is precisely why it can not be you. It is no sacrifice if a life is not extinguished...permanently."

Tears again filled his eyes as his pain clouded his judgement. "She will hate me."

"She never has to know. We'll tell her the child died. It happens all the time. Two of her own children were stillborn. One died in her crib. It won't be a terrible shock." She stood and looked the body over, seeing the soul start to slip away. "It is up to you, my love, but it is the only way and if I am to save her, I must do it now."

He stood, looking from the baby to his daughter. "If you do this, how long will she live? Twenty years? Thirty? Or will she succumb to sickness in a few months and this was all for nothing?"

"Forever," she promised. "I'll take not just the life force of the child, but of all future generations that would have been. An infinite number of souls will fuel her existence. She will never have to leave us."

"Forever? Are you sure?"

"Only an act of God will be able to snuff her out."

He looked down one more time at the child in his arms before handing her over. "All right," he agreed, wiping the tears from his face. "Do what you must. Just bring my daughter back to me."

He left the tent, unable to watch what came next. He looked in on his three granddaughters sleeping soundly in their own tent a few yards away. Allydia would survive the loss of the child for the sake of the others. Most importantly, *she would survive.* He walked back, warming himself by the fire, glaring at his son-in-law who was still somehow not quite dead. He paced, hands on his hips as he waited. Finally, Lilith stepped out of the tent.

"It worked. Just, not exactly how I intended."

"What does that mean?"

"As I was doing the spell, I discovered that the child would only have three generations after her. Our Allydia would die in seventy years. That was not what I promised you, so I improvised." She held a cup next to Farhan's neck and slit his throat, blood filling the chalice, the man already so close to death that he could not object. "This," she explained. "Will be what sustains her. The blood of others will replace food and drink. *Life* in liquid form. There will be side effects, but--"

"What kind of side effects?"

"Aversion to sunlight, firstly. It will tire her, make her weak. But, she'll be strong in the night. Almost as strong as me, and fast. Men will fall at her feet, catering to her every desire, of which there will be many. The hardest thing will be controlling her blood-lust. She will crave it like air and will do anything to get it."

He felt nauseous.

"Don't worry," she tried to reassure him. "I will guide her, show her how to use her new abilities and how to stifle herself when needed. She is back with us and that is all that matters, yes?"

He stared as she reentered the tent, watching in horror as his wife held the cup to his daughter's lips. She drank hungrily, her pupils dilating until the entirety of the irises had gone black.

He gasped and backed away. "Dear God, what have I done?" he whispered, crumpling to the ground and gazing into the fire. "Forgive me, Grandfather. My grief has made me a fool and a contributor to evil. I have made her a killer, just as I am, but worse. I am unforgiving and brutal but she will be a rabid animal, unable to be contained. She'll be something dark, born of the witch's black magic. I should have known better, Grandfather. I should have--" He stopped, the rustling from the children's tent snapping him to attention. He jumped up and ran to them, his still innocent granddaughters. They slept, unaware of what had befallen their family that night. "They won't be safe," he muttered to himself. His heart raced and his breathing quickened as he took them from their beds, gently as not to wake them. He piled them in the cart and made sure it was fixed tight to the donkey's harness. He led them away, fleeing the city, never to return.

Allydia pulled her sword from the fallen Nephilim and turned to face another as he barreled toward her. Stone-faced and with an exasperated sigh, she lifted her weapon and swung, slicing off her would-be attacker's head with minimal effort. She trekked up the hill to get a better vantage point and assessed the situation. The battle raged on, her vampires making quick work of taking down the Nephilim menace. As the torrent of rain poured, ankle-deep water mixed with blood caused a sea of red to rise over her enemies' bodies. She smirked as she began her descent. She'd won. But as she reveled in her presumptive victory, the dead began to wake. She looked on in horror as they stood, again reaching for their weapons and attempting their assault. She cracked her neck, raised her sword, and raced to the field. Just as she skidded to a stop in front of a seven-foot-tall Nephilim holding the severed head of her general, the rain stopped. The monster was gone. Her army had disappeared. The muddied battlefield was replaced by a rocky landscape with grass so green, she could see its brilliant color even in the moonlight. Before her was a lake mirroring the starry sky and in the distance, she could see a snow-capped mountain.

"What trickery is this?" she wondered aloud, taking in her new surroundings.

"Not trickery," a voice from behind her spoke. "I simply moved you, for your own safety."

She spun around to look her kidnapper in the eye. "Who are you?"

"My name is Gabriel. I'm an angel of the Lord your God. I apologize if I frightened you. That was not my intention."

"An angel? Like Lilith?"

"*Not* like Lilith."

"Why have you brought me to this place? Where are we?"

Gabriel appeared to take a deep breath as she looked around, though Allydia heard no sounds of life come from her. No heartbeat, no air moving through her lungs. It was as if the woman before her was made of pure light. The angel smiled. "They call it, 'Tarshish'. Beautiful, isn't it?"

"I demand you take me back. The Nephilim--"

"Are being handled."

"Handled?"

"It is not your fight," Gabriel insisted.

"It most certainly *is* my fight. Do you know what they have done? They consume everything they come across. They starve the humans, that is when they're not slaughtering them en masse. Those people are my people's food. Without them, we will die. That is why I declared war on the Nephilim scourge. I *must* defeat them."

"Worry not. My Father is purging them from the Earth as we speak."

She cast her a quizzical glare. "The rain?"

"The rain."

"But, everyone else. My people. The humans."

"A temporary loss. The souls will all be reborn, over time."

"Why spare me, then?"

"My Father commanded it. Your assistance will be required in a future altercation. Your stepmother will escape from her prison and He'll need you and an army of your kind to fight against her and those that follow her."

Allydia scoffed. "Why would I help Elohim in a fight against Lilith? He didn't save me from death, *she* did. He cursed my father. He let four of my children die."

"Three," the angel corrected. "He allowed *three* of your children to die. The fourth was not His doing."

"Thaddea--"

"Would have lived a long and healthy life. She would have had children and grandchildren. She didn't *die*. Lilith killed her."

She took a step back. "You're lying."

"I'm not. She would have done anything to prevent Cain from leaving her. She has a fear of being alone. Men give her a sense of stability. So, she brought you back as a gift to him, knowing that he wouldn't forgive her for allowing you to perish. She sacrificed the child in the spell that forced your soul back into your body."

"How could you know this?"

"I know anything God wants me to know. I'm His Messenger."

"So, does He want me to know this? So I'll help Him?"

"He wants you to know the truth. What you do with it is up to you, but there *is* an incentive."

Allydia folded her arms and raised an eyebrow.

"Your father took your daughters. He married them off and they were lost to you. Generations have passed and you have no way of tracking their descendants. But, God does. He knows where they are and if you help Him--"

"He will tell me." Her features softened and tears began to form in her eyes.

"In a few thousand years, I will come to you again. I'll look different and my speech will be riddled with expletives as I'll be born as a human, but my knowledge will remain. I'll tell you then that the time has come for you to do your part. When Lilith and her soldiers have all been defeated, I will give you the location of your remaining descendants. I won't know until the war is over, but as soon as I do, I *will* tell you."

She wiped away a stray tear and looked the angel over, her oddly pale skin seeming to glow and her fiery hair somehow still in the cool breeze. "I accept Elohim's terms. I will help Him."

"In that case, I look forward to our next meeting."

"Dia," a voice whispered in the dark. "Dia, wake up." The light came on, jolting the vampire from her sleep. She knew without opening the curtains that it was still day.

"Who dare--"

"It's me, Gabriel," the woman said, sitting next to her in her bed. "It's time to get this party started."

"Messenger?" Allydia asked, looking the woman over. "You *do* look different."

"I know, right? I was going for a whole ethereal, otherworldly thing back in the day. Thought it would drive home the point, you know? Me angel, you Jane. Sorry to wake you up and everything, but if I tried to sneak in here at night, somebody would *definitely* try to eat me, and not in the fun way." She handed her a piece of paper. "This is my number. Lilith hasn't Shawshanked it just yet, but when she does, she'll be bringing a bunch of demons with her, so keep an eye out and call me if you see any. Nice club. Reminds me of high school, all goth and shit. I was more of a hippy myself, you know, hemp necklaces, flannel. Now, though, I alternate between classy and sophisticated and tight jeans and band T-shirts. Depends on my mood. Anyway, it's a nice little empire you've built for yourself. I'm gonna skedaddle. The sun'll be down in about five minutes and I don't want to be here when the creepy-crawlies wake up. Have some fun tonight. Relax. Pretty soon, things are gonna get bloody and not in the way you like."

She watched Gabriel leave the room, scowling as she set the paper on the nightstand. She'd had almost five thousand years to rethink the decision to aid God in his battle against her stepmother. She'd gone over it again and again and the more she'd thought about it, the angrier she became. Lilith murdered her youngest daughter and her father had stolen the rest. They should both be in the ground as far as she was concerned. Now, finally, her chance at revenge on her stepmother was soon at hand. She leaned back into her pillows, a wicked grin creeping across her face. She took the brush from the drawer and ran it through her hair as she said to herself, "Not long now."

Chapter 1

The bullets whizzing by as she crouched behind a display of snack cakes didn't faze Yara, a decade on the force having given her nerves of steel. Her partner had the lookout cuffed and was using him as a shield as he barked orders at the two gunmen, one shooting at the officers from the center of the store and the other with a gun to the clerk's head, demanding to be let go.

"Drop your weapons!"

"Suck my dick, pig!" the first gunman shouted, again shooting in his general direction.

"Drop your weapons, now!"

"We just wanna get out of here," the second man said. "We don't wanna hurt nobody."

"Could've fooled me," Officer Jackson said, his eyes plastered to the first shooter.

"That's just Popcorn," the lookout told him. "He ain't been right since cops killed his daddy."

"Why you sayin' my name, bro?"

"Why you shootin' at *cops*?"

"You on their side?"

"Yo, I didn't sign up for this. Y'all told me this was 'bout to be easy money. You said there wasn't even bullets in your guns."

"You bought that?" the officer chortled.

"Hey! No one's talking to you!" Shots rang out again, bullets bursting bottles of wiper fluid and bags of chips as the clerk squeezed his eyes shut in fear. The gunman had had enough. He only had a few bullets left and he wanted to make them count. He strode out of his hiding spot and raised his weapon, shooting Officer Jackson in the shoulder and busting out the glass of the door behind him. The officer dropped his gun and fell back, losing his grip on the lookout.

"Fuck this," he said, running from the building, hands still cuffed behind him.

"Not so talkative now, are you pig?" Popcorn stood over the policeman, gun cocked, but before he could pull the trigger, a shot rang out from behind. He went to turn around but realized he couldn't. He'd been hit. He fell, blood soaking through the back of his white tee-shirt, the gun clanking on the floor.

"Jackson, you all right?" Yara asked as she edged toward the counter, her eyes fixed on the remaining gunman.

"Yeah, Rocha, I'm fine." The officer sat up, covering his would and catching his breath.

"You look pale."

"I'm Black."

"You need an ambulance. Call it in, I got this."

"Stay back, lady," the gunman warned. "I'll shoot him, I swear to God."

"I believe you. Put down your weapon." She inched closer.

"I said stay back!"

"So, your friend's name was Popcorn. I have *got* to hear the story behind that."

"Lady,"

"Was he corny with a tendency of popping people or did he just really like movies?"

"Bitch, I said get back!" He turned his gun on her, releasing the clerk who dropped to the ground and covered his ears. Without hesitation, she mowed him down, emptying her clip into his chest. He fell in a heap next to the clerk who screamed and scurried away.

"A little excessive, don't you think?" Jackson commented.

"What?" She holstered her weapon, feigning innocence. "You saw him aiming at me. I was in fear for my life."

"You goaded him into it."

"Hey, if you commit a crime in *my* neighborhood, expect to pay."

He raised an eyebrow.

"You know what they say. Don't start nothin', it won't be nothin'."

"You're fucked up."

"I'm a cop. I do what needs to be done. You don't see him complaining, do you?" She pointed to the clerk, still shaking on the floor. "He was a criminal. As far as I'm concerned, he had it coming."

"Yeah, Chief?" Yara said, entering the police chief's office.

"Close the door, Rocha," he instructed, taking a sip of coffee. "Sit down, we need to chat."

She did as instructed, folding her hands in her lap as she waited for what was sure to be another lecture on excessive force.

"I read your report and I have some questions."

"Which report, sir?"

He took the file from a drawer and slid it across the desk. She opened it, pretending to skim it over when she knew full well which report he was talking about. "Ah, the convenience store robbery."

"Yes, the robbery that somehow ended with one of my officers in a sling, two suspects dead, and another in the wind. You want to explain to me what happened?"

"It's all in the report, sir."

He squinted at her and snatched up the file, putting on his reading glasses and clearing his throat before reading aloud. "*I told the suspect to put down his weapon. He did not comply. Instead, he turned it on me. I could see the safety was off and I felt that I was in immediate danger, so I reacted.*"

"Yes, sir."

"And that's all there is to the story?"

"Sir?"

"Your partner issued a report of his own. Said you provoked the suspect. Said you fanned the flames and that it could have gone down differently. Said it seemed to *him* like you *wanted* to kill that boy."

"That's ridiculous."

"Is it? Because this isn't the first time something like this has happened. This isn't even the first partner of yours that's come to me with concerns."

She rolled her eyes. "Sir,"

"That boy was seventeen, did you know that?"

"No."

"He was a *kid*. I've gotten a dozen calls today from people demanding I investigate. They want the surveillance and bodycam footage released to the public. His parents will probably sue. Do you have any idea the position you've put this department in?"

"I understand."

"Do you? Because I'm looking at you and you're cold as ice. You have no remorse. You don't give a--"

"My partner was down. He was about to get killed, so I had his back. When he was safe, I focused on the last perp. The kid had a gun to an old man's head and told me he'd kill him. What should I have done? I had three choices: let the suspect go, let the old man get killed, or take the shot. I took the damn shot. Yes, it's sad that he wasn't *quite* an adult, but come on. He was a criminal and if I'd let him off the hook--"

"I don't want to hear any more. You're suspended pending an investigation, but if I were you, I'd hire a lawyer and start thinking about career options."

"Are you serious?"

"You see a brick wall behind my head? Yeah, I'm serious. Gun and badge."

She scoffed as she stood, shaking her head and placing the items on the desk. "I can't believe this. After everything I've done for this community."

"I'm not discounting the work you've put in, Rocha. I'm telling you you've gone too far, *again*. Maybe you should get some help."

"Help? Like a shrink? You think I'm crazy?"

"I think if a medical professional could testify that you weren't in your right mind when the incident occurred, you might avoid jail time altogether."

"Jail time? I'm sorry sir, but are you on crack?"

"Get out of my precinct, Rocha."

She stormed out of the office, slamming the door behind her and ignoring everyone in the building as she made her way out, their self-righteous stares like daggers in her back. Ten years she'd dedicated her life to this place, to these people, to this city. *Ten years.* Her mind raced as she walked home. Should she try to fight this? Try to get her job back? Or should she track Jackson down and give him a talking to about ratting out your partner? Maybe she should say, 'fuck it', buy some fertilizer, and blow the whole precinct to shit. She took a deep breath, cracking her neck as she tried to calm her mind. "The point is to stay *out* of prison," she whispered to herself. But thoughts of revenge lingered. She imagined shooting the chief between the eyes, setting pipe bombs, and watching as people she once called friends get blown apart in a fiery shower of blood and broken badges. She thought about breaking into Jackson's apartment and wrapping her hands around his rat-fink throat until his eyes popped out of their sockets and he passed out. Mostly, she thought about the kid and how good it had felt to put all those bullets in him. Seventeen or not, she was glad he was dead. "One more criminal off the streets."

"You talkin' to me?" a man asked as she passed. She shook her head and kept moving, a sly smile creeping across her lips. Yes, she was glad the boy was dead. Her only regret was that his friend, the lookout, had gotten away. She was sure she'd see him around the neighborhood, eventually. She was looking forward to it.

Yara jumped at the sight of a man sitting on her couch as she opened the door. On instinct, she reached for her sidearm before remembering that it wasn't there. "What do you want?"

"To talk," the man said, putting his hands up as if he was about to be arrested. "I would have waited outside, but this isn't exactly a safe neighborhood."

"Who are you?" She stayed in the doorway, ready to bolt if things got out of control.

"Come sit."

She scoffed.

He sighed and stood up, buttoning his suit jacket. "I really do just want to talk." She tried to back out of the room, but he was too fast. He grabbed her arm and pulled her inside, closing the door and standing between it and her. He put two fingers to his temple, gently massaging it for a few seconds as he looked her over. "I don't wish to harm you, Yara, honestly."

"How do you know my name?"

"I know all of my descendants' names. I've kept track."

"Your what? Man, who the hell are you?"

"My name is Cain. I'm your one hundred and eighty-first great grandfather. I was hoping we might--"

"So, you're not a burglar, you're a lunatic. All right, bro. Get out of my house."

He rubbed his temple again, this time closing his eyes and wincing.

"Hey, man, you all right? Listen, I'm sorry. Mental illness isn't a joke. But you can't just--"

"I'm not mentally ill," he insisted. "Why are you people always so quick to assume a person is out of their mind? Just because you don't understand something, doesn't make it insane. Let me explain. As I said, I am Cain, son of Adam, father of Enoch, Allydia--"

"Cain? Like, from the Bible? That's who you think you are?"

"*No*, that's who I *am*. Anyhow, my son, Olad, had children who had children and so on through the millennia until we come to you. I really didn't mean to frighten you. I would just like to get to know--" He reached up with both hands and held his head, gritting his teeth.

"Do you need an ambulance? I'm calling--"

"Don't!" he snapped. "This is just what happens when I stay in one place too long. Part of God's curse."

"God's curse? Bro, you're whacked. You need help. I'm calling someone."

She went for the phone in her pocket, but he grabbed her arm again. "I said, '*no*'." He flung her to the ground. "Please, believe me, granddaughter. *Please.* I want us to be friends. I want to know you. We're family, after all."

She glared at him, her anger from the day's events bubbling over. It would be irresponsible of her to go after the boys in blue, but this guy? He was an intruder. He'd attacked her. She had every excuse in the world.

She looked past him, just long enough for him to turn to see what she was looking at. When he did, she swept her leg across the back of his, knocking him to the ground. She leaped on top of him, punching him in the jaw before pressing down on his throat, using as much of her body weight as she could to crush his windpipe. He gripped her wrists tight, prying her hands off of his neck. Sure that he would overpower her, she switched strategies, kneeing him in the groin and jumping up, making a beeline for the door. Just as she was about to turn the knob, she felt the pain of her skull being cracked. He'd hurled something at the back of her head, causing her to drop to her knees. She touched her head and looked at her hand. It was covered in blood. The room seemed dimmer as she tried to stand, her legs not wanting to cooperate. Suddenly, she felt a sharp pain flood through her, starting between her shoulder blades and coming out her chest. She looked down and could see what looked like metal poking out from between her breasts. Blood flooded from her mouth onto the carpet as the weapon was yanked from her body. She fell forward, her head crashing into the door with an audible thump. Her vision had gone blurry, but she could just make out the silhouette of the man as he wiped her blood from something before placing it in what looked like a briefcase.

"I really didn't want to do this, Yara," he told her. "I was hoping things would be different with you. I'm starting to believe you're all the same. I can't tell you how disappointed I am in you." He left the apartment, scooting her across the floor as he opened the door, her vision now completely black. She couldn't feel anything anymore; not the pain, not the floor, not even her anger. There was just...nothing.

Outside, Cain set his case on the sidewalk and took a pen and a small, leather-bound notebook from his jacket pocket, opening it to the last page with writing on it. He crossed off the name *Yara Rocha*. There was only one name remaining. He put his things back in his pocket, picked up the briefcase, and took a breath. "Well," he murmured. "I guess I have a plane to catch."

Chapter 2

"I hate this," Wendy complained as she twirled Gabriel's hair between her fingers. "I wish I didn't have to go back to work already."

"You don't *have* to," she told her, gently pulling her toward the entrance of her building.

"I'm not taking your money."

"Come on, just a little. Ten million. You could quit your job and we could be on vacation all the time."

"As tempting as that sounds, I do actually like my job. Plus, I don't want you to think I'm taking advantage of you."

"Please, I know you're just in it for the sex," Gabriel teased.

"And the jokes."

"Well, sure. I'm pretty hilarious."

"I really have to go. I'll call you as soon as I get back."

"Fine, but I'm agreeing under duress."

"Noted." She kissed her and touched her cheek. "I'll see you later."

They parted ways, Wendy heading back toward the subway and Gabriel walking into her building alone. As she entered the elevator, she was struck with a familiar but overwhelming feeling. She was knocked to the ground by a flood of new information filling her brain, dropping her suitcase, and swallowing the bile that rose in her throat. She clutched her chest with one hand and searched for the railing with the other as she tried to catch her breath. The world around her seemed to spin and go dim. She managed to crawl to the front of the lift and hit the emergency stop button, ensuring none of her neighbors would stumble upon her in this state. She closed her eyes and took deep breaths, blowing them out her mouth as her organs vibrated, the power of what waited for her upstairs shocking her system. She sang 'Sherry Fraser' to herself as her body adjusted, having always found the melody soothing. She finally got her bearings and was able to stand, putting her hand to her forehead as her mind cleared. She hit the button for her floor and readied herself. "Get it together, bitch."

The doors opened and she found Michelle sitting in front of her apartment. She stood up and threw her arms around her neck. She was trembling as Gabriel hugged her back. "I didn't know what else to do," the girl said. "I don't trust anyone but you."

She pulled away and picked up a blanket that had been covering the car seat. Gabriel held back tears as she looked down at the baby resting peacefully, knowing that maintaining her composure was vital under the circumstances.

"Come in," she said, unlocking the door. Michelle picked up the carrier and followed her inside, locking the door back behind her. "I thought you were dead."

"I'm not *not* dead," the vampire joked, setting the carrier on the island and stepping back. "Will?"

Gabriel shook her head.

She swallowed the lump in her throat. "I figured. Is his dad okay?"

"Okay's maybe a stretch. He's alive, taking care of himself. He'll be all right."

"You know why I'm here."

She nodded, looking down at the infant.

"And you know what the Queen will do if she finds out a damphyr has been born, much less one with Nephilim powers."

"I do know."

"Hattie said nothing on Earth is stronger than a human/vampire hybrid. Is that true?"

"Usually."

"I took the morning-after pill."

"I know."

"I don't want you to think I was irresponsible."

"Girl, I see you."

"Yeah. So, you'll take her?"

Gabriel sighed.

"Do you know what the punishment for a vampire siring without permission is? I'll be thrown in a cage until Allydia can track Hattie down. Once she does, she'll make her kill me before yanking her fangs out with pliers and chaining her on the roof just before sunrise. If she finds me with Sinclair, she'll drown her in front of me. That's what I named her, Sinclair, for her father. I thought about Willa or Willow, but when I saw her face, Sinclair just felt right."

"It suits her," she said, letting the baby grab onto her finger.

"Hattie won't leave Scotland and without her, I'm having a really hard time controlling myself." She glanced at the baby and back to Gabriel. "She smells like food."

"Jesus, yes, I'll take her. Here," She took a key from the junk drawer and handed it to her. "Go to the house in Southport. B's all moved out, so it'll be empty, except for the furniture." She rifled through her purse, found her wallet, and pulled out a credit card. She gave it to her and touched her arm. "I'll send a steady stream of blood bags so you can ride out the new-vampire urges without killing anyone. Call me if it gets too bad and I'll rush right down."

She nodded. "Thanks. And you'll protect her, right?"

"Her whole life." She picked up her phone and texted the pilot to have the jet gassed up. "The plane will be ready to go by the time you get to the airport."

Michelle wiped away a tear as she took one last look at her baby. "Will she be okay?"

"She'll be perfect. And, yes, I'll tell her you love her and you gave her to me for her own safety. I promise she'll understand."

"How do you know?"

She gave her a condescending glare. "Who am I?"

She laughed. "Right."

"I'll have a box of blood waiting for you when you get to the house."

"Okay." She turned to leave.

"Michelle,"

"Yeah," she said, grasping the doorknob.

"I'm glad you didn't stay dead."

She smiled and nodded, opened the door, and left.

As the door closed, Sinclair let out a quiet cry, again reaching for Gabriel's finger. She picked the baby up and held her close to her chest, rocking back and forth, letting the tears she'd been stifling fall down her cheeks. She sang 'Golden Slumbers' as they cried, the child's broken heart more painful to Gabriel than the loss she'd felt when Raphael had gone back to Heaven. The child wanted her mother and the only thing Gabriel could think to do to ease her suffering was to give her a new one.

Wyatt ran his hand over Allydia's forehead and down her cheek as he kissed her, indulging in her body for the third time that night. It had been two weeks since the battle for the Gate and in that time, the two had barely left the bedroom, worshiping each other and blocking out the world around them.

Yo! he heard in his head.

He stopped what he was doing and grimaced. *Not now, Gabriel.*

When your girlfriend leaves, book it to my place. It's urgent.

"What's wrong?" Allydia asked.

"Nothing," he said. *Bye, Gabriel.*

Say 'okay'.

Fine, I'll see you in the morning.

K, bye.

"Well, that's over," he huffed, rolling back to his side of the bed.

"Your sister?"

"Yeah. Apparently, there's some big emergency."

"Isn't there always?" she quipped, pushing the hair away from his eyes.

He chuckled.

"Speaking of your sister, there's something I need to talk with you about."

He raised an eyebrow.

"There are things I haven't told you, not because I wanted to deceive you, but because it's hard for me to think about. You asked me once why I hated Lilith so much."

"I remember."

"I told you it was because she took something that didn't belong to her."

He nodded.

"What she took, what she snuffed out, was the life of my youngest child. She murdered her as an infant in order to make me what I am."

"Jesus."

"I did not ask for this life. I was fine with dying when I did. But my father could not endure it. Lilith manipulated him into allowing her to bring me back this way because she was afraid of being without him. When he saw what I'd become, he was worried that I would harm my daughters, so he stole them away. As much as it pained me, in retrospect, he was probably right."

"God, I'm so sorry. That must have been awful."

"It was. But, years later, Gabriel came to me, saved me from your Father's flood. She told me that one day, she would come again and call on me to aid in a battle against Lilith. In return for my assistance, she would give me the location of my daughters' descendants. Earlier this evening, she sent me two addresses."

"She found them?"

"Not so much found as was gifted with the knowledge. I would like to see them."

"Of course. You should."

"I don't want the others to know where I've gone. There's talk of rebellion among my people. If my enemies discover I have human family, they could use them. They could hurt them. They wouldn't dare attempt to harm *you*. Word of your abilities has spread. They fear you. But humans...I can't risk it. I need to go on my own as not to raise suspicion."

"Sure, go ahead. Take as much time as you need."

She touched his face and stared into his eyes. "Will you be all right?"

"I'll be fine," he assured her, taking her hand in his and kissing it. "This is your family. You *have* to go. I'll be okay, I swear."

"Thank you." She got up and put her clothes back on, slipping the wispy sundress over her head and pulling it down around her. "Hartley will be at your disposal, should you need anything. I've already told her to treat your calls as if they were mine."

"That's not necessary."

"Perhaps not, but it brings me comfort knowing she's watching over you when I can not."

"You don't have to treat me like I'm made of glass."

"So you say, but my heart still breaks remembering you floating in the tub."

"I'm sorry about that," he said, sitting up and pulling her to his lap.

"I know you are." She wrapped her arm around his shoulders and touched his chin. "And I *will* learn to give you your space, in time. But, for now, while I'm away, I'd like to enjoy myself instead of worrying about your safety. Can you understand my perspective?"

"Yes," he sighed. "I suppose I can. As long as *you* can promise to start trusting me."

"I will." She got up, slipped on her shoes, and headed for the door. "As soon as I get back."

Chapter 3

"All right, I'm here," Wyatt called as he entered Gabriel's apartment. "What's the big problem *now*?" He closed the door behind him and walked to the living room where he nearly tripped over the baby lying on a blanket in the middle of the floor. "Oh, sorry, sweetie," he cooed, kneeling down and tickling the child's stomach. "I didn't see you there." She giggled and grabbed his hand.

"Hey," Gabriel said as she appeared from the hall.

"Hey," he said, standing up. "Cute baby. I'm a little surprised somebody's letting *you* babysit."

"Haha."

"Who is she?"

"You should sit."

"Why?"

"I recommend sitting."

"Gabriel," he prodded.

"Barachiel," she mocked.

"Who is she?"

She furrowed her brow and folded her arms.

He tilted his head and raised his eyebrows.

She rolled her eyes and sighed. "She's your granddaughter."

He laughed. "She's what?"

"Michelle brought her to me. Turns out, Hattie snuck some of her blood to her before Will zapped her. She was pregnant when she turned."

His face went ghost-white and his mouth fell open. He turned to look down at the infant playing happily with a rattle. He knelt back down and covered his mouth as tears began to form in his eyes. "That's not possible. She would have only been pregnant for, what, two months?"

"She's not exactly human, B. The rules on what consists of a normal gestation period don't really apply." She sat next to him and patted him on the back. "Michelle can't keep her.

She's not in control of her vampire shit, yet. She thinks she might hurt her. I'm gonna give her to Uriel."

He flashed her a look. "The hell you are. She belongs with *me*."

"Listen, B,"

"No," he said, getting to his feet and pulling her up by the arm. "I know Valerie wants a kid, but you can't just--"

"*Allydia will kill her*."

He dropped her arm and took a step back.

"This kid isn't normal, B. She's what the vampires call a 'damphyr'. Stronger than vampires, able to walk in the sun, can survive on blood *or* normal food. Your girlfriend has rules about stuff like this. *Laws*."

"She wouldn't."

"I know her a lot better than you do. Trust me on this. Dia will drown her, tear her to pieces, and burn the parts to ash. *I've seen her do it*, and that was with regular damphyrs. One with lightning-controlling Nephilim powers? She might put her through a meat grinder just to be safe."

He stared at her, horrified, his mind racing.

"If you leave, she won't spiral into a depression again. This time, *she will hunt you*. Besides, I know how you feel about her."

"What," he choked. "What do you mean, 'Nephilim powers'?"

The baby giggled and grabbed his ankle, sending a small jolt of electricity through his jeans, causing the hair on his leg to stand up.

His eyes widened as he looked down at her and back to his sister. "Already?"

Gabriel bit her bottom lip and nodded.

His throat went dry and his voice quivered. "Will she be okay, or is she like...is she--"

"She'll be fine." She picked her up and handed her to him. "She'll age fast. Faster than Will. She'll have some growing pains, but eventually, she'll be good as new."

He held her in his arms and couldn't help but smile through his tears. "She's perfect."

"I know, right? Oh, Michelle named her Sinclair."

His face brightened.

"I thought you'd like that."

"Wait," he worried. "Where's Lucifer? If he even *thinks* about--"

"Settle down. He's been shacked up at the bartender's place for days."

Wyatt's shoulders relaxed, but his jaw was still tight as he looked down at his granddaughter's smiling face.

"You can visit any time," Gabriel comforted. "Just make sure it's during the day."

"So," he said, tears again threatening to fall from his worried eyes. "Sinclair Perry?"

"Maybe Sinclair *Ann* Perry, for her grandmother."

Tears streamed as he nodded and took a shaky breath.

"Ann happens to also be *my* middle name, but that's just a happy coincidence."

He laughed and the baby giggled and kicked her legs. "I think she likes it."

"She doesn't care about her name. She just likes seeing you happy."

Wyatt turned his glance back to his sister. "You know that?"

"Obvs."

"I thought you couldn't see--"

"She's not the same as Will. Not exactly. Just like you and Lucifer and Uriel, I can hear her thoughts, feel her emotions. I'll always know what she needs and she can call on me whenever. Trust me, you don't have to worry about her. She's gonna be awesome."

"And you're sure Valerie can handle this?"

She scoffed. "That bitch can handle *anything*."

"Spider, spider!" Valerie yelped, pointing to the ceiling and backing away.

Malik chuckled as he took the stick vac from the hall closet, plugged it in, and proceeded to suck the tiny creature into it."Demons, monsters, and Lucifer you can handle, but one little bug, and you're heading for the hills."

"Not *all* bugs. Just *those* things, *especially* when they're up high. They can fall and get in your hair and get stuck." She shuddered. "I don't even want to think about it."

He laughed, put the vacuum away, and kissed her cheek. "I'll be gone for a couple days for that class, but when I get home, I'll have a dozen new recipes in my repertoire. Think about what you want for my first dinner back *now*. I don't wanna have the 'I don't know, what do you want' conversation for half an hour *again*."

"I mean, *okay*, but just so you know, we probably will."

He laughed again, picking up his suitcase as he left, waving goodbye and closing the door behind him. She sat down on the couch, crossed her legs, and looked around the apartment. She tapped her fingers on her knee and began to chew on her bottom lip. It had been like this since she'd gotten back from Iraq. With no job and no monsters to deal with, she didn't know what to do with her time. There was no urgency. Nothing needed done.

She flopped her head back and let out a frustrated sigh. *"I'm so bored."* She picked up the laptop from the coffee table and searched job listings with no luck for the third day in a row before putting the computer back in annoyance. Just as she was about to get up to mindlessly snack on something to pass the time, the door flew open. From the hall, she could hear Gabriel singing 'Circle of Life' as an empty car seat floated into the room.

"The fuck?" Valerie muttered.

Soon, her sister appeared holding a baby up in front of her, still singing, a goofy smile on her glossy lips. She closed the door with her mind and handed the child over, unable to stop herself from giggling.

"Aren't you the cutest little light-skinned baby ever?" Valerie said, looking down at the gleaming infant. She instinctively began rocking back and forth as she turned her attention to her sister. "What kind of moron let you watch their kid?"

She folded her arms. "Okay, this is getting insulting. Just because I'm not *parent material*, doesn't mean I'm irresponsible. I can take care of a baby for a *day*."

"Uh, huh. For real, whose kid is this?"

She looked her in the eyes and did the floss before answering, "Yours."

She raised her eyebrows. "Girl, did you kidnap this baby?"

"No, jeez. Let's sit." They moved to the sofa, Valerie bouncing the girl on her knee. "So, her name's Sinclair Ann. She's Barachiel's granddaughter."

Valerie tilted her head and widened her eyes.

"I know, right? So, you know how Will was boning Michelle, but then he accidentally killed her with his emotional-break-down-lightning?"

"Yeah."

"Well, while Hattie had been helping train her to protect herself before she went to Southport, they became real good friends."

"Hattie's the vampire's assistant, right?"

"Was. So, apparently, when Will started showing signs of going dark side, Michelle had her overnight her some of her blood. She put a little in her orange juice every morning. Grody, I know. So, instead of staying dead, she turned. Unbeknownst to her, she was knocked up at the time, and that's how our great-niece came to be."

"That's a different level of fucked up."

She shrugged.

"All right, but I can't keep her. She should be with Wyatt. He's--"

"Banging a vampire."

"Yeah, but--"

"Sinclair isn't human, Uri. She's half vampire, half Nephilim. Dia will *slaughter her* if she finds out she exists. I went over this with B. He gets it. He doesn't *like* it, but he gets it. He knows the only place she'll be safe is with you."

"What about me? What about Malik? Are *we* safe with *her*?" She looked down into the baby's seemingly innocent face. "No offense, cutie, but my man's just a dude and you're--"

"Family," Gabriel insisted. "She's our family, Uri. She's got no one else."

She went quiet, thinking about the years in foster care, the loneliness, and the trauma. She remembered the abuse.

She looked her sister in the eyes, warmth washing over her as she remembered how grateful she'd been when she'd brought her to her grandmother. She knew she was just trying to do the same thing for Sinclair now. "You're right," she said, smiling down at her new daughter. "She can stay here."

"Good. There's formula in the bag. If you run out, she can drink blood in a pinch, but she'd really rather not. Also, the diapers I have are size one, but she'll outgrow those in a couple days. I'll just send over some supplies."

"A couple days?"

"She's gonna grow fast. Like, 'take-a-ton-of-pictures-because-you'll-forget-what-she-looked-like-from-one-day-to-the-next' fast."

"Wait, did you say, '*blood*'?"

She got up and headed for the door, twirling her hair as she went. "Yeah, it's not important."

Wyatt sat on the grass of his wife's grave, his back against the headstone, eating the candy bar his sister had given him on his way out the door. He hadn't realized how hungry he was until now, having skipped breakfast in his rush to get to Gabriel's. She did, though. She always knew.

"It's been a while since we've talked. I know you can't hear me, I'm not *crazy*...turns out. I just need some perspective. I thought if I came here, got some things out, I might feel better about this whole absentee-grandfather thing. *Grandfather*. That's so weird." He took another bite and leaned his head back, watching the clouds as he chewed. He stretched his legs out, crossing one ankle over the other as he finished the candy, crumpled the wrapper, and shoved it in the pocket of his jeans. "I should trust Gabriel here, right? She always knows what she's doing, except maybe for that whole theater incident. I'm still not sure how much slack I should cut her there. On one hand, those people were possessed and probably wouldn't make it, anyway. I saw her when Tae died. She wasn't okay. Doesn't seem like much of an excuse, though, does it? I mean, she hasn't shown *any* remorse about it and that's just weird, right? I don't know. Maybe it's different for her, being God's taskmaster, knowing what He wants from her and the rest of us, what He *expects*. It's probably a huge burden, knowing all the big picture stuff. Fifty lives is a drop in the bucket to someone like that. Plus, constantly having other people's thoughts in her head can't be exactly peaceful. Feeling everyone else's emotions. I'm surprised she hasn't cracked up more often. Still." He tore up a bit of grass and let out a breath. "Valerie will be a good mom. She's worked with kids for years, she'll be fine...I hope." He ran his tongue over his back teeth and folded his arms. "There's something else I wanted to talk to you about. There's this girl. I don't know *what's* going on. It's completely unhealthy, codependent, potentially dangerous. There's something about her, though. She makes me feel needed and wanted. She looks at me like I matter. Like I'm the only person in the world. She makes me a priority. I don't know if anyone else has ever cared about me like that. I feel like I need her. It's insane. I don't know, maybe I *am* crazy. I wish you were here. I could really use my best friend right now." As he stood to go, a gentle breeze rustled his hair, the scent of lavender wafting by, ever so briefly, the air like a kiss on his cheek. He looked around, trying to figure out where the smell was coming from. The cemetery was deserted but for him and the landscaper, and of all the flowers on graves he could see, none of them were Annie's favorite. He kissed his fingertips and touched the headstone. "I should really get back into therapy."

Chapter 4

Cain sipped his brandy, admiring the view from the small window of the plane. He looked down at the Atlantic through the wisps of clouds, noticing how peaceful the world seemed from this altitude, nothing but an ocean of blue below him. He imagined that's what Heaven must be like, not that he'd ever get a chance to know that now. His plan had failed. His curse remained.

He straightened his tie and cleared his throat, pushing away the anger and closing his eyes as he composed himself. He needed to be pragmatic. He took a deep breath and cleared his mind, letting the magazine that he'd been reading fall to the floor.

"Here you are, sir," the flight attendant said, hurrying to pick it up and set it on his tray. "Can I get you anything?"

"No, thank you," he replied, meeting her gaze and feigning a smile.

"All right. Enjoy the rest of the flight."

"Actually," he said. "What's your name?"

"Wendy."

"Hi, Wendy. Could I get another brandy? I've almost finished this one."

"Of course. Give me one second." She smiled sweetly and scurried off to fetch his drink. He watched her go, his lips turning up into a devilish smirk. The angels had destroyed his only chance at breaking God's curse, and while he had no way of doing them any physical harm, he *would* make them suffer for it.

Poe set her basket down on the soft grass, the heat of the afternoon sun making her rethink her decision to wear patent leather pants and a black tee-shirt to do the day's gardening. "Ah, well," she shrugged. "Already writing the ticket." She reached up and bent the stalk of the first mullein flower down, being careful not to break it, and plucked off its buds and flower spikes one by one, dropping them into her basket. She moved on to the next one, the six-foot stalks nearly a foot taller than her, reminding her, as Grace always had when they were harvesting, that she was one small part in a much bigger universe.

As she went for her third flower, she heard a rustling in the grass just past the garden. She brushed her short, dark hair away from her eyes with the back of her hand and squinted in the harsh daylight as she went to investigate. She covered her mouth and gasped when she came upon it, the small, brown and white rabbit, convulsing on the ground.

"What happened, baby?" she wondered. "What did you--" And then she saw it: purple flowers, some half-eaten, strewn across the grass a few feet away. "Foxglove. Oh, shit." She scooped the bunny up and hurried back to the house. "Sorry about the sticky fingers, cuteness. Don't worry. We'll get you fixed right up. I promise." She kicked open the screen door and rushed in. Once in the kitchen, she dumped the apples from the bowl on the table and set the bunny inside. She then got to work, pulverizing as many bayberries as she could using a mortar and pestle. Once she was satisfied with the consistency, she used a needleless syringe to administer the medicine to the rabbit. Within seconds, it began vomiting. "Good job, buddy," she cooed as she pet its fluffy back. When she was sure there was nothing left in the animal's stomach, she went to the pantry and found the jar marked *activated charcoal powder*. She dumped some in a bowl with a little water to make a paste and used a clean syringe to feed it to the bunny. She then fed it some water through the syringe and gave it a bath in the sink, the animal too weak to put up a fight.

For the next few days, Poe nursed the rabbit back to health, feeding it water with the syringe and holding out pieces of kale for it to munch on until it could lift its head and feed itself. She held the bunny close on her chest when it slept to make sure it was breathing and when it seemed to be on the mend, she bought a bale of hay and a collar with a bell on it so she'd always know where her new friend was. She let it roam the garden, thinking that, eventually, it would wander off, never to be seen again. But it never did. It stayed with her, sleeping in her bed, hopping along wherever she went. It was the best friend she'd ever had.

"I'm gonna call you 'Raven'," she told the bunny, petting it as it ate from its bowl on the kitchen table. "You can stay with me as long as you want, but if you ever want to go, I'll respect your choice." As she watched the bunny eat, she realized that she was smiling for the first time since Grace died. It had been strange, living in her house without her; lonely and sad. But, having a pet had given her purpose and she was finally on her way to feeling like herself again.

Poe was in the garden gathering herbs when she heard a noise coming from inside the house. She thought Raven had knocked something over, so she went in, expecting to have a mess to sweep up, but what she found would take a lot more than a broom to clean. Julia and two other witches from her coven were standing in her kitchen, rifling through drawers, and emptying jars of herbs. There were piles of powders and dried leaves all over the counters and Grace's recipe cards were scattered across the table. Julia stood over them, flipping through the pages of a spellbook she'd found in a cabinet.

"What the hell are you doing?" Poe shouted, frantically looking around the room.

"It's none of your concern," Julia told her, not looking up from the book.

"The hell it's not. I live here!"

She sighed, closing the book and folding her arms, finally meeting Poe's gaze. "We're looking for Grace's magic. She hid it from the coven. It's not right. It has to be here somewhere."

"It's not."

"It *has* to be."

"I'm telling you, I live here and I don't feel it anywhere."

"What part of, 'she hid it' is confusing to you? Grace was the most powerful witch I've ever known. If she didn't want something found, there is no way someone like *you* would be able to find it."

"Someone like me?"

Julia rolled her eyes. "Don't get offended, you know what I mean. You're young, barely trained."

"Personally trained by Grace herself. I'm not as weak as you seem to think I am."

"You're a child, but, fine. Let's say you're as strong as the rest of us. It means nothing. Without the Tituban magic, we're all as good as dead."

"You still think the other covens are coming after us?"

"Not yet, but they will be. I don't know about you, but I don't want to be a sitting duck. Look, I'm sorry about the mess, but this is important." She looked the girl over. "You and Grace were close. Like, mother and daughter, close."

"So?"

"So, are you *sure* you don't know where she put her magic?"

"She didn't tell me. I was as surprised as you when it didn't pass to us."

"When it didn't pass to *us*," She put her hands on her hips. "You mean the coven?"

She nodded.

"You know, we've been working under the assumption that Grace didn't bother choosing someone to take her place, but what if she did? What if she cared so much about you, that she wanted *you* to take over when she died?"

Poe scoffed. "*Me?*"

"Not the obvious choice, of course," Julia said, tapping her fingers on the spell book's cover. "You're the youngest member of the coven, the least experienced. But, she did love you. We could all see it. She fawned over you like a pet. She would have known that the rest of the coven would hate it if she left you in charge, especially the elders. Can you imagine Libby's face if Grace had told her that her eighty-year-old ass would be taking orders from *you* from now on?"

The other women laughed.

"But, if she left all of her magic to you, *just you*, we would have no choice."

Poe swallowed hard. "I don't have it."

"You don't?"

"No."

"How can you tell?"

"What do you mean?"

"Grace could have hidden it in you, dormant, until you needed it. You wouldn't even know it was there."

"That's crazy."

"Is it? Let's find out. Quassatura."

Searing pain ripped through Poe's arm as a deep scratch opened up across her skin. "Ow! What the fuck, Julia?"

"Well, damn it. I thought I was on to something."

"I told you, I don't have it. It's not here. You're wasting your time."

"Maybe you're right," she huffed. "But, if it's not with you, the only other place it could be is--"

"The elders," another woman said.

Julia nodded. "But, why would they keep it from the rest of us? Why wouldn't they use it? Doesn't make sense."

"Did you ever think that maybe Grace hid it to protect us? You know how powerful she was. What if it's too much for us?"

"Too much? We're *witches*."

"Yeah, but--"

"But nothing. That power belongs to the coven and I'm *going* to find it."

She stomped out, the other two following closely behind. As the door slammed shut, Raven popped out from under the sink, hopping over and sitting at Poe's feet. The young witch picked up the rabbit and sat in a chair, hoping to be comforted by its affection. But, she couldn't shake the feeling of dread twisting in her stomach like a knife. Julia was out of control and something bad was going to happen. She could feel it.

Chapter 5

Allydia perched herself on the roof of the building across from the first address Gabriel had given her, a one-bedroom flat in the heart of Camden Town. It had been some time since she'd visited London and as she waited, she wondered if Queen Mary's Rose Gardens were as beautiful as she remembered. She first saw them in 1934, the day they opened to the public. She remembered thinking how worth it it was, being out in the daylight, to see such vibrant colors. She'd only stayed a short time, of course, but she could picture it in her mind even now. She'd be sure to stop by for a stroll before she left.

Her ears pricked up at the sound of a doorknob turning. She watched as the door to her descendant's building opened and a man walked out. He was in his late-twenties to early-thirties with dark hair and a skin tone that resembled her own. He was slender and tall, wearing khaki cargo pants and a plain, black tee-shirt. As she focused her vision, his face became clear, even at this distance. He was clean-shaven with full lips, and even though she was sure it was impossible, she would have sworn on her life that he had Farhan's eyes.

He walked for a few blocks, Allydia hopping from one rooftop to another as she followed. He stopped in front of a shop, but before he could open the door, it burst open, an older man bounding out to meet him.

"Navid!" He slapped him on both shoulders, a wide grin peeking out from his full, gray beard. "So good of you to come. Are you well?"

"I am," he replied. "And you?"

"We're wonderful, thanks to you. Business has *tripled* since you got those hoodlums off the street. Come, come. Shadi has a gift for you; her famous bamieh, to say 'thank you'."

"Bamieh?" the younger man asked, placing a hand on his stomach. "Well, let's get inside before I start drooling all over the pavement."

The men laughed and went in, the door closing slowly behind them. Allydia crouched down, trying to get a glimpse inside, but there were too many people. It was a party of some sort, inside what looked like a bakery. There was a counter and a glass case full of pastries, a few tables, and a sign on the door that read, 'closed'. It was loud inside, at least two dozen voices talking all at once. She'd lost track of him for now, so she'd wait, the early evening sky quickly turning dark giving her the cover she needed. She stared at the door, anxious to get another look at him, to compare his features with her own. "Navid," she whispered to herself, the sound of his name like a warm blanket around her shoulders. She wondered what his life was like. He was obviously beloved by the people in his community and from the conversation he'd just had, she assumed he worked in law enforcement. Was he happy? Content? She couldn't leave until she knew.

After more than two hours, Navid emerged, waving to the other party guests and carrying a tin. He began the short walk home, taking a pastry from the container, and eating as he went. Allydia again followed, shimmying down the side of a building and sticking to the shadows on the sidewalk across the street. The scent of rose water and saffron wafted from his hands as he closed the tin back, reminding her of something she'd eaten as a child. She thought those memories had been all but lost to her, her human life having ended so long ago. A lump formed in her throat. It was all she could do to stop herself from tearing up.

As Navid approached the door to his building, he stopped, looking around as if he knew he was being followed. Allydia slunk back into an alley, out of sight, or so she thought. In her excitement, she'd forgotten the way her eyes shone in the dark, reflecting what little light was available. For a short time, the presence of a blood relative had made her forget what she was; not only inhuman, but a predator.

He looked across to where she stood, unable to see anything through the dark but her eyes, yellow and glowing.

She could hear his heart skip a beat as he swallowed hard. He rushed to get inside and bounded up the stairs to his apartment, nearly dropping his pastries as he hastily got the door unlocked. Once safe, she could hear his breathing steady. She felt a twinge of guilt for frightening him, but couldn't resist the urge to keep following. She *had* to know he was all right.

She crept across the street and climbed up the side of the building, looking in windows until she found him. She could hear him on the phone reporting a strange animal sighting. He thought he'd seen a lion or cougar stalking him on the quiet city street. The man on the other end of the call laughed but said he'd send someone to check it out. As she listened, she took note of his surroundings. A small sofa served as the only seating in the living room. Two bar stools stood in front of an island with one cushion far more worn than the other. In the bedroom, there was a nightstand on one side of a twin-sized bed. He clearly lived alone.

Her eyes again fell to him. He wore no ring, so he had no wife. The only pictures she could see were of an older couple who she assumed must be his parents, though neither bore any resemblance to him. No other photographs could only mean that he had no children that he knew of. It seemed that he led a solitary life, with work and friends taking up most of his time. He was relatively young, so she didn't jump to any conclusions about how that affected his happiness. She, though, was ecstatic to see him, offspring of her offspring, alive, healthy, and thriving.

He set the phone on the counter and turned toward the window, Allydia able to hear his heart beginning to race. She skidded down to the sidewalk and darted across the street, clawing her way up a building and again crouching down to watch him from afar.

Navid hid in the tall shrubs, watching with intense concentration as the woman walked through the gardens, stopping for a time to admire the Boy and Frog statue. It was early in the morning, but the temperature had already risen to nearly seventy degrees Fahrenheit, and yet, the woman was almost completely shrouded in a heavy cloak. Who was she? He had to know.

Chapter 6

Once in Tripoli, Cain headed straight for an apartment building near Saint Vasilios Square where he knew the last of his descendants took residence. She was a sixty-year-old retired nurse and while she wasn't his first choice, she was all that was left.

"Yes?" She said in Greek as she opened the door.

"Hello," Cain replied. "Are you Dimitra?"

"I am. And who might you be?"

"My name is Cain. This may sound crazy, but I think we're related."

"Oh! You've done one of those DNA tests, haven't you?"

"Something like that."

"Well, come in! I'll make tea." She showed him in and headed to the small kitchen. "Have a seat. We can tell each other stories. I've been alone for so long, it's wonderful to know I have family out in the world. Where are you from? I can't place your accent."

He sat on the couch, set his briefcase next to him on the floor, and placed his hands on his knees. "I was born in what they call Iraq, but I've traveled all over since then. I've lived on every continent except Antarctica, though if things don't change for me soon, I may end up there, as well."

"That sounds exciting," she said, setting two cups on the coffee table and joining him on the sofa. "I must tell you, your Greek is perfect. So, you travel for work?"

"Sometimes. Mostly, I just feel compelled to move on from one place to another...frequently. You might say I'm forced."

She raised her eyebrows and sipped her tea. "So what is it that you do?"

"For work?"

She nodded.

"I sell antiques, some antiquities, mostly at auction. When you're as old as I am, you tend to accumulate a lot of unnecessary trinkets. It's quite lucrative."

She snickered. "You think you're old? What are you, late-thirties? You're a baby." She patted his cheek before putting her cup back on the table.

"I'm older than you think."

She gave him a condescending glance.

"By thousands of years."

Her face fell as she saw the seriousness in his eyes. "How did you say we're related again?"

"Dimitra, there's no reason for you to be nervous."

"All right," she said, putting some distance between them on the couch.

"I am Cain, son of Adam, banished by God from my home, never able to create another for myself. *You* are my last living descendant."

She stared, her heart pounding.

"Good," he smiled. "The others laughed, at first. They didn't believe me. But you do, don't you?"

"I don't know what to believe." She took another sip of tea, the cup clinking against the glass of the table as she put it down, her hands trembling. "It sounds insane, but,"

"But?"

"There is something familiar about your face. In the cheeks and around the eyes. So much like my father's. When you said we were related, that's why I believed you. You must be a cousin."

"I'm not."

"I am a religious woman, but,"

"Look in my eyes, Dimitra. *Look at me*. Do you think I'm lying to you?"

A shaky hand covered her mouth as she looked him over.

Relief washed over him. "Good, that's good. Thank you, granddaughter. You're the first to see the truth. I've spent *millennia* searching for *one* to understand. You've made me very happy today."

"What do you want from me?"

"What I've always wanted. *Family*. One that wouldn't hate me for abandoning them when God's curse compelled me to leave. One that would remember me."

She could feel how tense her muscles had become. She took a deep breath and tried to relax, but her body wouldn't cooperate. "How can this be true? If you are who you say you are, how can you still be alive?"

His expression went dark as he remembered. "God punished me with eternal life when I killed my brother. He cursed me with the inability to stay in one place. I *need* to leave, sometimes after two weeks, sometimes twenty years. I get an urge, like a drowning man longing to breathe. I've tried forcing myself to stay put, but that ends in..."

"In what?"

"Bloodshed. I lose control. I lose my sanity. I slaughter those I love."

She stood and backed away.

"I won't hurt you, Dimitra. I swear it."

"You just admitted to *killing people. Your family.*"

He stood and walked toward her. "Yes, but it won't happen with you."

"How can I know that?"

He thought for a moment. She was older, not exactly someone he could take along on his travels. He couldn't stay with her, of course. Besides his curse, he had revenge to take. "You're right. You have no reason to trust me. I'll go." He picked up his case and went to the door. As he turned the knob, he suddenly got excited. "We can exchange letters! You can keep me apprised of your life's happenings. I can tell you all about my adventures, send you pictures of the places I go, things I see. We'll be pen-pals. I'm off to America next. New York. I'll send you something Statue of Liberty related." He smiled from ear to ear, the joy he felt in his heart like nothing he'd experienced before, at least, not that he could remember.

"All right," she agreed, her hand on her chest.

"Thank you, granddaughter. You have no idea what a blessing you are to me." He closed the door behind him as he left, the smile still plastered on his face. *Finally*, he thought. *A real family.* But she would only live another thirty years, at most. She would have no children. Soon he would be alone again, this time with no hope of ever being anything but. As he stepped out onto the pavement his anger returned. He'd spend as much time as he could visiting and corresponding with his new-found granddaughter, indulging in the love of family for what little time she had left. For now, though, he would have his vengeance.

Chapter 7

Michelle sat cross-legged at the top of the staircase, running her hand over a spot on the carpet still slightly tinted pink. The floors had been cleaned, but she could still smell the blood through the chemicals; Will's blood.

She had held herself together in front of Gabriel, but now, as she stayed alone in his house, the memories of her lost love had her reeling. Hattie had explained that her emotions would be amplified, but this was overwhelming. Her chest was tight, her stomach hurt, her head pounded. Her entire body ached for him. She couldn't sleep because every time she closed her eyes, she saw him, covered in blood, holding the knife to his throat, his bottom lip quivering. It must have broken his heart, living with what he'd done to her, even if for only a short time. She knew it had been an accident. He wasn't in control. She would have given anything to tell him she was okay and that she understood. The truth was, she would have forgiven him anything. She loved him with her whole heart and nothing, not psychosis, murder, or death could change how she felt.

Tears spilled down her cheeks as she lay down on the stained carpet, breathing in what she could of his scent. She sobbed, digging her nails into the soft floor and allowing the quiet cries to escape her throat. She didn't know how she'd go on, but she would. Somehow, she would get herself through this because she knew in her soul that Will would have wanted her to.

"I'm back!" Malik called, entering the apartment and dropping his suitcase at the door. "Val? Val, you home?" He looked quizzically at the baby-gym on the living room floor and the high-chair in the dining room. "You went shopping?"

"In here!" she called back.

"A little soon to be--" he stopped in the doorway to what used to be the guestroom, now decorated as a full-blown nursery, a crib against one wall, a changing table on another, and in the corner by the window sat his wife in a rocking chair, holding what looked to be a six-month-old baby in a pink onesie. "What's this?"

"We need to talk."

"I see that." He knelt next to her and took the infant's small hand. "Who's this?"

"Sinclair," Valerie told him, smiling down at her and back at him. "Sinclair Ann Perry."

He looked up at her, his eyes wide in surprise and confusion.

"Gabriel brought her to us. *For* us...to raise."

"Your sister, what?"

"She's my great-niece, Will's daughter."

"Will? The half-angel psycho that lost his mind and killed a bunch of people?" He felt a small jolt of electricity zap his hand. He pulled it away from Sinclair's grip and stood up. "What the..."

Valerie giggled. "I guess she doesn't like you talkin' shit about her daddy."

"What the hell is she?"

"*Be nice*. She's part-angel, part-vampire, part-human. One hundred percent family."

"Val, we can't...I mean, this is..." His voice trailed off as he folded his arms, furrowing his brow as his mind raced.

"The fuck we can't."

"Shouldn't Wyatt take care of her? She's *his*--"

"If the vampire he's fuckin' finds out she exists, she'll put her in a wood chipper. If Lucifer finds out, same thing. Gabriel's not exactly down for diaper duty, so we're it. This child has got no one else. Yes, she's a little complicated, but--"

"Val, she just *electrocuted me*. And, did you say, '*vampire*'?"

"Gabriel promised she's harmless. This isn't up for debate. She's *our* baby now. Only question is, what kind of father are you gonna be?"

The statement took him off guard. His jaw clenched and his heart leaped to his throat. He could tell she was dead serious. He would lose her if he didn't act right *quick*. So, he pushed his concerns aside, relaxed his arms, and softened his features. "I'm gonna be the best dad I can be." He knelt back down and pinched the infant's cheek. "But no more shocking me, okay?"

She giggled.

He laughed, too. "Awe, you're a good baby, huh? You eating real food, yet?"

"Still on baby food," Valerie said.

"Well, I make a mean sweet potato/banana puree. Maybe carrot applesauce? Just wait for those teeth to come in. You'll be eatin' real good."

The baby giggled again.

"You sure you're okay with this?" Valerie asked.

"Do I have a choice?" he chuckled.

"No."

"I'm cool with it. You're right. She's family. Besides, she's a baby. What's the worst that can happen?"

Michelle slurped the last few drops of blood from the final bag that Gabriel had sent. It should have been enough to last a week, but she was insatiable, emptying the stash in three nights. She was restless and tired of mourning. All she did was sit in the silence of her dead lover's house, missing him and thinking about their daughter. She knew giving her to Gabriel had been the right thing to do. There was no doubt in her mind about that. Still, she couldn't get the image of her face as she left her out of her mind. She looked so heartbroken. Like she knew. Michelle obsessed over that night, and the twisting guilt in her stomach mixed with her grief over Will had her mind swirling. She needed to get out of this house for a while. She needed to get away from herself.

She texted Gabriel, *Need more blood.* She immediately got a text back that read, *On its way.* It would be the next night before it arrived and while she knew logically that she should wait it out, her instincts were telling her something different. She was crawling out of her skin and she was hungry.

    She decided to take a walk. The warm, late-summer breeze felt soft against her skin as she tied her long curls up in a scrunchie, her short sundress blowing lazily around her legs. She'd walk along the road for a while before turning back and going into the woods to hunt. Maybe she'd get lucky and find a deer or two. If nothing else, a rabbit or a squirrel might be enough of a snack to hold her over until her next shipment of human blood got there. Just a short walk, then a quick hunt. That was the plan. However, after only just losing sight of the house, a truck pulled up next to her.

    "Get in," the driver demanded.

    She sighed as she saw the man's face. It was the creep that had harassed her at the bowling alley the night Will first started slipping. It was his fault. If he hadn't provoked him, threatened her, Will never would have snapped. *He would have been fine*, she thought. *Everything would have been fine*.

    "Bitch, I said get in." He slammed on the breaks and got out of the truck without turning off the engine. He stomped toward her, his jaw and fists clenched.

    "You really should be running," she warned.

    "You should be screaming," he retorted, reaching out to grab her by her ponytail, but before he could make contact, she grasped his wrist, twisted his arm behind him, and swept his leg out from under him, knocking him to the ground. He yelped in pain and surprise.

    "I told you to run." She snapped his arm, the satisfying cracking sound sending a chill up her spine. He cried out, another sound she relished. She could hear his heartbeat quicken and feel his pulse speeding up under her thumb. He was afraid and she loved it.

    "Let go of me you crazy bitch!"

    "Let go? Is this not what you wanted?" She flipped him onto his back and swiped her nails across his cheek, leaving four perfect lines of blood dripping onto the pavement. The smell of it sent her into a frenzy. She was losing control. Her eyes flashed in the light of his high-beams and he gasped.

"What the fuck are you?"

"I'm a wild animal dressed like a princess. You wanted me in your truck. Let's get in the truck." She lifted him up by his collar and threw him, one-handed, into the driver seat. She was a blur to him as she sped around to the passenger side and slid in. "What's your plan, cornbread? What did you think would happen once I was trapped in your car?"

He held his arm, holding back tears as rage, pain, and terror mingled on his face. "I was gonna play with you a little first, but now I'm just gonna kill you."

She laughed, holding her stomach as she bellowed. "You're gonna *what*? Oh, man, that's amazing. Oh, Jesus, I can't tell you how much I needed that. Thanks for the laugh, buddy, really. Much appreciated." She continued to cackle as his face went red.

He moved closer in a sad attempt to overpower her, but she grabbed him by the throat and shoved him down into his seat. "You know," she remarked. "I've had a real shitty past few months. Like, *the worst*. I blame you. Maybe that's ridiculous. Maybe things would have gone sideways no matter what. But I'm putting it on you. Your fault. You fucked it all up. And, yet, I was willing to walk away, be the bigger person. I tried to tell you. I said, 'run'. Did you listen? Of course not. You're a sociopath. Serial killer? Racist? It doesn't matter. You're bleeding now and I'm starving, so." Her eyes dilated and her fangs grew. He screamed, using his good hand to try to push her away. She slammed it into the door before pressing his head to the side, exposing his neck. Her skin felt hot as she caved to her instincts and bit down, gulping mouthfuls of the warm, salty fluid that escaped his veins. He fought against her, kicking and pushing, but she was too strong. His squirming became weaker as she drank and when he'd lost too much blood, he passed out. She kept drinking, unable to stop herself. Eventually, she felt his pulse on her lips stop. His heart went quiet.

She pulled back and looked him over, her belly full and her eyes and teeth returning to normal. She felt no guilt for what she'd done. She knew she should, that it was horrible not to. Monstrous. But in that moment, all she felt was justified.

A flash of light drew her attention to the windshield. Another car was approaching. She hurried out of the truck and rushed to the field beyond the road, hiding in the tall stalks of corn. She watched as the car stopped and a man got out to investigate while a woman in the passenger seat waited.

"Call nine-one-one!" the man yelled. The woman complied as the man felt the corpse's wrist for a pulse. Michelle scurried away, unnoticed by the pair. She ran straight back to the house, locking herself inside. She washed the blood from her lips, nose, and chin, threw on a pair of pajamas, and went up to Will's old bedroom. If the police came, she'd say she'd been sleeping and didn't know anything about what happened to the stranger just down the road.

Chapter 8

Wendy dropped her bag and kicked off her shoes. The last few days at work had been exhausting and she was glad to finally be home.

"Hello, Wendy," a voice said from the dimly lit kitchen. "Don't be startled. I'm a friend of your girlfriend."

"Are you?" she asked, unconvinced, recognizing him from her flight to Greece a few days before. She walked toward the man, showing no fear, which seemed to surprise him.

He took a knife from a drawer and spun it on the counter. "Oh, yes. We go way back. Several times over the years I asked God to lift the curse He placed on me. Begged Him. And every time, Gabriel would come to me and say that He would not. No explanation, just refusal."

"God cursed you? Doesn't sound like Him."

He smirked. "You should reread Genesis."

"And you and Gabriel are friends?" she condescended.

"Well, maybe not 'friends'. But I *do* know her. She's not the only person we have in common. I believe you've also met my daughter, Allydia."

She tilted her head as she put together who he must be. "Cain?"

"In the flesh."

"Huh. I thought you died like, five thousand years ago."

"Would that I could."

"Uh, huh."

"You see, I had a plan. Destroy the Gate to Heaven and kill the angels, thereby severing the link between God's consciousness and Earth and in turn, breaking my curse. I would be free to settle, marry, and have a family. I would grow old and by the time God woke and repaired the Gate, I would have been long dead, my soul in Purgatory, on its way to being reborn. I could have been a normal man, Wendy. I could have had *a life*. But the angels robbed me of it."

"Okay, but didn't you like, brutally murder your brother over some bullshit? Seems like you had the whole curse thing coming."

He slammed his fist down on the counter. His jaw tightened and a low growl escaped his throat. He dabbed the sweat from his brow and collected himself before addressing her again. "My brother and I had come to an amicable distribution of the world's resources. He would rule over the creatures of the Earth and the land would be mine to cultivate. I grew olives, figs, and pomegranates. I had fields of barley and wheat. I grew melons bigger than your head, and when I offered my finest crops to Elohim as a tribute, he rejected them. But my brother slew a few lambs and *that* was considered a proper sacrifice. I was jealous of my brother and couldn't control my resentment." He paused, picking up the knife and gazing into it like a mirror. "When He asked what I'd done, I lied. *That's* what He hated. He didn't care that Abel was dead. He was angry that I attempted to deceive Him."

"Cool story, bro. So, why are you here, exactly?"

He set the knife down and closed the distance between them. "The angels stole my chance at happiness. Snatched it from my hands just as I was reaching for it. So, I will take from them what gives them joy, starting with you." He reached for her throat, his face twisted in a maniacal grin. But before his fingers could touch her skin, he was thrown back, slamming into the dining table and falling to the floor.

"Yeah, I should have told you," she said. "When I helped save the Gate from your lackey, I also took the warding your ex had given him. Technically, being immortal and all, you're a supernatural creature. You can't hurt me. Although, if I'm being honest, if you were just a dude, I would have kicked your ass pretty hard, anyway, because spells."

He picked up the knife and hurled it at her face, but it bounced off an invisible shield that seemed to surround her. He took the spike from its case and stomped toward her, but when he got close, he was again sent flailing, crashing hard into the upper cabinets and dropping down to the gray, slate tiled floor.

He stood, brushing off the sleeves of his suit jacket and letting out an angry sigh. He huffed past her and left the apartment, muttering under his breath, "*Witches.*"

Allydia stood in the empty apartment, her brows furrowed as she placed her hands on her hips. It felt suspicious. She'd called Gabriel to confirm the address and she'd told her that, indeed, one of her descendants did live there. But there was no one. The only things left were a few scattered papers on the floor and two teacups sitting on a glass coffee table, still mostly full of what smelled to her like Sideritis and honey.

She walked through the rooms, wondering what had happened, why someone would have left in such a hurry. She hoped whoever had resided there was all right and that she'd be able to track them down one day.

"You're back!" Gabriel gleaned as she ushered Wendy into the apartment. She hugged her tightly and kissed her, her excitement clear on her face.

"I'm back," Wendy smiled, taking her girlfriend's hands in hers. "I have to tell you something. That Cain dude showed up at my place today."

She bit her lip and cupped Wendy's face in her hands, "Are you okay? You don't look hurt."

"No, I'm fine. Lilith's warding. He can't touch me."

She let out a sigh of relief. "Right. Good. Okay. Maybe you should stay with me for a few days, though, just in case."

"I can take care of myself. He's pretty pissed we ruined his master plan, though."

"Yeah, but you know what they say. While we make plans, God laughs and says, 'Not so fast, dumbass'."

"Oh, is that how the saying goes?" she snickered.

"That is *totally* the unredacted version," Gabriel giggled.

They kissed again, allowing their hands to run over one another's bodies. "Lucifer here?"

Gabriel shook her head. "Still with the bartender."

"Well," she slipped her fingers into the waist of her lover's jeans and pulled her closer, fiddling with the top button. "Maybe I could stay *one* night."

Chapter 9

Lucifer brushed his lips along the side of Mariana's neck as she buried her face in her pillow, reaching back and taking a fistful of his soft, blond hair in her trembling hand. She moaned in aching pleasure as she submitted, the pressure of his body on her back, dominating her like a hungry beast sending chills up and down her spine. She couldn't get enough of him. He was a drug and she was addicted.

"Am I hurting you, love?" he asked, his voice quiet and husky in her ear.

She opened her mouth to answer, but her mind was too clouded by bliss to form words, so she shook her head and steadied herself on the mattress as she began to climax. As they finished, light from the rising sun filtered through the rose-colored blinds of Mariana's window, illuminating the small bedroom in a pinkish hue. Lucifer stood, finding his slacks and swiftly pulling them on.

"What are you doing?" She clicked the lamp on and pulled the blanket up around her.

"I need to stop by my sister's for some fresh clothes and a shower."

"You can shower here."

"Yes, but I've been wearing the same trousers for three days. It's obscene."

"On the rare occasion that you're actually wearing pants," she teased.

He flashed a flirty smirk, kissed her cheek, and finished dressing. "Would it be too forward of me to pay you another visit tomorrow?"

She smiled, getting up on her knees and letting the blanket fall. She sucked on her bottom lip and ran her hand over his chest. "I'd be offended if you didn't."

"Very well." He gave her a once over, held her face in his hands, and kissed her hard. "I will see you soon." He left the room and the apartment, making sure to lock up before closing the door, and heading down the stairs.

The early morning air was still as he began the long walk to Gabriel's apartment. The quiet of the usually busy street allowed his mind to wander. He thought about the time he'd spent with Mariana and how relaxing it had been. He'd never been on Earth long enough to develop an attachment to a human before. He wasn't sure what he was feeling, but he *did* know that he'd grown fond of her company and was looking forward to seeing her again. Perhaps he'd follow in his sister's footsteps and open up to Mariana more. Not about who he really was, of course, but maybe a conversation where both parties were fully clothed wouldn't be the *worst* thing.

"Coming!" Wyatt called as he hurried to pull up his jeans and throw on a tee-shirt, the sound of persistent banging on his door waking him from a too-short sleep. He rushed to answer it, not recognizing the man standing before him. "Yes?"

"You call yourself 'Wyatt', yes?" the man asked.

"That's my name."

"Is it? My ex-wife told me something different. Unless you're *not* the angel that wields lightning?"

He glanced around the hall to make sure none of his neighbors had heard. It was empty. "Who are you?"

"My apologies. I should have introduced myself sooner, considering you're sleeping with my daughter."

Wyatt raised an eyebrow and stepped aside, allowing the man to enter. "Allydia's not here. I expect her back tonight, though. I can tell her you stopped by."

"That won't be necessary. I know not to attempt a visit with her during daylight hours. I came to see you."

"If you want to know what my intentions are, I honestly couldn't tell you. Coffee?" He poured two cups, relieved to have a coffee maker with a timer. He wasn't twenty anymore and staying up into the wee hours was beginning to take a toll.

"I'd love some, thank you."

"How do you take it?"

"Black as my soul."

Wyatt snickered as he handed him the cup and gestured toward the barstool across from him.

Cain sat, taking a sip and setting the drink down on the smooth countertop. "It's very good."

"Filtered water," he said, gulping it down and pouring another cup. "A trick my son taught me."

He tilted his head. "You have a son?"

"Not anymore."

He sat up straight. "Well, my condolences. I know what it's like to lose children."

"I'd imagine."

"Yes. Speaking of children, I came to warn you of one of mine."

"Warn me?" He wiped the sleep from his eyes and did his best to focus on what Cain was telling him through the fog of exhaustion.

"I've watched my daughter over the years, hoping that as she learned to control her urges, she'd return to her once sweet-natured ways. You should have seen her, helping me in the fields, tending to her children. She was a light in the dark for me. But the years have made her hard. She's grown sadistic. My fault, if I'm being honest, either by my actions or sheer genetics. Either way, it would be in your best interest to flee from her before she turns her anger to you...and kills you."

He chortled. "As long as she's alive, I can't die."

"'Alive' being a relative term."

He sighed and folded his hands. "What are you doing here?"

"As I said--"

"You're trying to get me to leave my girlfriend, your own daughter. You hate her that much?"

"I don't hate her," he insisted, his jaw tightening. "*I miss her*. It killed me to abandon her."

"And kidnap her kids?"

"I did what I had to!" He slammed his hand down on the counter, his face turning a deep shade of red. "You didn't see what I saw. *She was gone.* The witch brought her back with the darkest of magic and made her a creature I didn't recognize. She would have butchered those girls had I not saved them from her clutches."

"So, you're not just immortal. You're also psychic."

"Be glib all you like, but I was right. It broke my heart to do it, but *I was right*." He calmed down and took another sip of coffee as Wyatt stared daggers.

"You should go."

He looked him in the eye and sat back, breathing a sigh of defeat as he looked the angel over. "She's dangerous."

"I know that."

"But you won't heed my advice. She's gotten her hooks in." He squinted as he studied his face. "You love her." He stood, drank the last of his coffee, and walked back to the door. Taking the knob in his hand, he turned to address Wyatt one more time. "You're a damn fool."

Cain's attempt at killing two birds with one stone had failed spectacularly. The angel, Barachiel, had very few people in his life that he cared about and they were all other angels, aside from Allydia, who was also too powerful for him to take down. Breaking up their romantic relationship was all he could think to do to punish them for what they'd done. They'd have to go unscathed, for now.

Enraged by his second failure, he turned his attention to an easier target. He bounded up the steps to the apartment Lucifer had been spending so much time in lately. He was certain there was a woman inside; a *human* woman, weak compared to the others and perfect for taking out his frustrations on.

He made his way to her door and kicked it in, breaking the frame and sending bits of wood flying. She screamed, jumping back and running to the bedroom where she tried to lock him out. But he was too strong and pushed his way in with ease.

"You're quite pretty," he panted, already tired from physical exertion. "I'm not surprised. Lucifer always did have excellent taste."

Mariana grabbed the lamp from the nightstand and raised it, but as she brought it down, Cain caught it, avoiding a head injury and becoming more irritated. He threw it against the wall and shook his head, setting his briefcase on the bed, opening it, and pulling out the iron spike. She tried to run, but he grabbed her by the hair, yanking her back and tossing her to the floor. He stood over her, his heart beating out of his chest. He felt exhilarated, the panic on the girl's face like a jolt of caffeine. Finding her body would surely anger God's favorite son. It might even make him a touch sad. Cain laughed as he gripped the spike, lifted it up, and plunged it into the girl's heart.

She gasped, blood bubbling up and spilling from her quivering lips. He pulled his weapon out and stuck her again, this time in the abdomen. He smiled gleefully as blood splattered across his face. He stood upright, wiping his instrument on her bed-sheets and placing it back in its case. After a few seconds of convulsing, the girl's body went limp, her hands dropping to her sides, and the light in her eyes going dark.

He turned to the makeup table, using a tissue to clean his face. As he looked in the mirror, he wondered how he'd make sure Lucifer would know it was he who'd laid out this fantastically brutal scene for him to find. He tapped his fingers on the whitewashed wood and looked down. That's when he saw the makeup brushes and smiled.

Chapter 10

"I'll be back in a few days," Wendy giggled as Gabriel pet her hair and stuck out her lip.

"Fine, but next time someone calls in sick to a flight to goddamn *New Zealand*, fake a cold, maybe."

"I'll try." She kissed her goodbye and left the apartment.

"Well, it was nice seeing your significant other again, even if only for a few minutes," Lucifer said from the sofa. "Seems things are going swimmingly."

"Yeah, it's going great. Makes me feel like something bad's gonna happen any minute."

"Don't be so pessimistic, sister. She adores you, I can see it in her eyes. What could possibly go wrong?"

She gave him a knowing look. "All the things."

"All right, what's bothering you? Something's on your mind, I can tell. What is it? Barachiel in another depression? Did Uriel's husband leave her? Did one of your favorite reality stars get the clap?"

She laughed. "That would be hilarious, but no. I've recently been made aware of something and I'm struggling with it."

"Do tell." He sat across from her at the island, his interest piqued.

"I have to do something. It's not optional, it's God mandated. Gabriel knows it's the right thing to do. *Gabriel* understands."

"Ah, but *Taran Murphy--*"

"Can't bring herself to do it."

He folded his hands and leaned forward. "My advice, should you be willing to hear it,"

She nodded.

"Take your time. You know as well as I do that you will do as He commands. You will always aid our Father in his endeavors. It's how you were made. But, if it's hard, procrastinate." He gave her a wink and sat back.

"I don't think I should. I'd like to, I really would, but he's already attacked Wendy. He could come after any--"

"Who did?"

She sat down, folded her arms, and crossed her legs, a look of aggravation on her face. "Cain. He's in town and on the warpath. I guess he's salty we fucked up his big plan."

He rolled his eyes. "*Cain.* He's been a thorn in my side for years. Recent events aside, he used to follow me when I'd be here on the hunt for demons. Seems he thought we should be allies of some sort. He was a pest, always trying to endear himself to me, bringing me gifts, as if my friendship was somehow useful to him. That all changed when he found me with his daughter in Akrotiri. I'm not sure if he was offended that I'd bedded her or if he was simply so afraid of her that he decided not to risk another encounter. Either way, I was free of him after that."

She shot him a look. "Why would you put that image in my head? I already have to see that shit every time B's around. At this point, I feel like *I've* been fucking her."

"I'm surprised you haven't been."

"She only likes dudes."

"Oh, that's right."

"You hungry? I'm making dinner."

"You're *what*?"

She picked up her phone and showed him the restaurant's website.

"In that case, yes, I'm famished."

Chapter 11

Allydia sat on her throne, relieved to be back in the city she called home. She rifled through the papers on the small, marble table next to her, deciding none of it was worth her time. She was excited to get back to the apartment…to Wyatt.

"Your Majesty," her assistant said, bowing as she entered the room.

"Yes, Hartley, what is it?"

"How was your trip, my Queen?"

"It was fine."

"Your dress is beautiful. I especially like the corset. The black really brings out your--"

"Why are you stalling?"

"I apologize, Your Majesty. I hate giving you bad news."

"What is it?"

"While you were away, I personally kept watch of your lover at night, as you instructed."

"Yes?"

"And during the day, I had my most trusted human stake out his place. I told him that if anyone suspicious came around, to take a closer look and make sure nothing happened."

She sat up straight, her cold stare giving Hartley chills.

"He's fine," she assured her. "I went as soon as the sun went down myself to look in on him. I made sure he didn't see me. He was eating something from a box, looked like pizza. I have someone there now, just in case, but I thought I should show you this myself." She approached her, keeping her eyes averted as she pulled up the photos on her rhinestone-encrusted phone. "My man got pictures of a guy going into his apartment. Now, it's been a few decades since you showed me the portrait in the basement, so call me crazy, but is that the same man? Is this," She pointed to the face on the screen. "Is he the man you told us to avoid at all costs? That he was too dangerous? Is *this* the only man you fear?"

She studied the picture, squinting to get a good look. When she was certain, she stood up, the quickness of her motion startling her assistant, nearly causing her to drop the phone. "Fear has been replaced with indignation. Yes, that's him. And you're sure Wyatt's all right?"

"Yes, Your Majesty." She swiped the screen a few times and showed it to her Queen. It was a live feed of Wyatt, still sitting at the kitchen island, finishing a soda. It was clear that the video was being taken through a window with a zoom lens as the quality was somewhat grainy but clear enough to ease her mind.

"Good. Did your man follow the man in the picture?"

"No, he stayed watch, but he did send someone else. From what he told me, dude's kind of a psychopath."

"And you know where he is now?"

"Yes, my Queen."

She stomped to the door, her leather boots clicking on the wood sounding like urgency mixed with rage. "Text me the address."

She moved through the crowd like wind, fast, squeezing past vampires without them noticing. The music was loud and so were they, laughing and singing along as they drank. The lights were dim, but she could still make out the familiar shape of the man she'd only recently been stalking. She halted, tilting her head in confusion as he rushed up to her, vampires licking their lips as he passed.

"Why were you following me?" he accused. The eyes of the crowd turned to them.

"You shouldn't be here," she warned. "It isn't safe for you."

"I can handle myself. Who are you?"

She grabbed his arm and sped him out of the club, not stopping until they were several blocks away. She pulled him into an alley and folded her arms like an exasperated parent. "Why are you here, Navid?"

"What the hell? How did we get here?"

"Navid."

"How do you know my name? Why were you following me?"

She shifted her weight from one foot to another and sighed. "I'm impressed that you found me. I'm normally much better at covering my tracks."

"I'm a detective. Hunting people down is in my blood."

"Yes, I suppose it is."

"So, who is it, mm? O-Tray-One? ABM? Who sent you and what for? To kill me? Take your shot, but I warn you, I have no problem defending myself, even against a woman."

She chuckled. "You're feisty."

"I mean it. If one of them white boy gangster wannabe's has a beef and are too chicken-shit to come at me proper, deciding to send a girl to do their dirty work--"

"I would never hurt you, Navid. No one sent me."

He stepped back, the anger in his expression turning to confusion. "What, then? Woman as beautiful as you wouldn't be interested in a nobody bloke like me, definitely not to the point of criminal following. You a debt collector? I owe nothing, but you never know with identity theft being what it is."

"Nothing like that. I just wanted to get a look at you."

"What for?"

She peeked her head around the corner to make sure they hadn't been followed before looking him squarely in the eye. "We're related. Very, *very* distantly. I wanted to make sure you were all right. That's it. I promise, from now on, I will leave you alone."

"Related? How? That doesn't make sense."

"I have to take care of something and as I told you, you're not safe here. I need you to leave." She left the alley and didn't turn back, not wanting anyone who may be watching to see them together.

"But I have questions!" he called.

She quickened her steps. "Go home!"

Allydia opened the door to the first-floor hotel room, easily breaking the lock and startling the man inside. "Hello, Father."

He jumped up from his spot on the edge of the bed and backed away, catching his breath as he tried and failed to hide his terror. "Daughter."

"When was the last time our paths crossed? Do you remember?"

"It was 1583, The Battle of Torches, I believe."

"That's right. You came upon me feasting on a half-dead soldier and proceeded to vomit all over your boots."

"I remember."

"You scolded me. You called me a monster, said I was no daughter of yours. You told me that if you ever saw me again, you'd kill me. I believed you."

"Allydia, you must understand--"

"So, I kept my distance. I hid from you. I created a network of spies to inform me of your whereabouts to avoid you at all costs, and now you're here, in my city. Why? What have you been up to, Father? Besides harassing the man I love."

"Love?" he chortled. "Honestly, daughter. *Love*? He's not fit for *you*. One day, he will see you for what you are and he will run from you, if you don't destroy him first."

"You lost the right to an opinion on my love life when you murdered my husband."

"I faulted Farhan for your death, you can hardly blame me."

"Why are you here, Father?" she barked.

He jumped. "To bring justice to those that wronged me."

She tilted her head and folded her arms.

"*The angels*, girl. I had a chance at a normal life. If the Gate had been destroyed, if the angels were back in Heaven, the link between God and Earth would be severed. His power would no longer reach me. I would be able to have more children, age, and die. By the time He woke from his slumber, I would have been reborn, or at least, on my way to it. I'd be able to settle on a farm somewhere, live a life. It's all I've ever wanted. *A family.*"

She scowled, fighting the tears that threatened to come as she clenched her teeth. "You lost your chance at a family when you left me."

"I didn't leave *you*," he said, his voice shaky. He took the spike from the case. "My daughter was already dead." His words were stern, but his heart was racing, and beads of sweat formed on his temples. He was afraid of her, a realization that both saddened and amused her.

"The plow you used to slaughter your brother? It's a little melodramatic, don't you think?"

"I'll give you one chance to leave. You know you can't hurt me."

"And you know that's not true."

"Allydia,"

"I absolutely can. I shouldn't. There's a slight difference."

He backed away again, his back almost to the wall.

"I wouldn't kill you, of course. But there are other ways of making you suffer. Apply pressure here, remove an organ there."

"Allydia ibnat Cain."

"No ibnat!" she shouted, rushing toward him. "Calling me 'daughter' is another right you lost long ago."

He swallowed hard, tightening his grip on the iron spike. "Fine. But I did not lose all hope of family when you died. There's another. I met with her. We are to be friends. So, your angels didn't take *everything* from me. I will have a few decades with--"

"The woman in Tripoli?" she asked, stepping back.

"How did you know that?"

"I stopped by her apartment. By any chance, did she serve tea when you visited?"

His face fell. "What did you do?"

"I did nothing. She was gone by the time I arrived. The only things left were two teacups, still half full. She must have left in a hurry. I believe you frightened her."

"You're lying."

"You know I don't lie."

He fumed, nearly shaking in his anger.

"Seems you are alone, Father. As God intended." She opened the door. "Stay away from Wyatt. If you come near him again, I won't hesitate." She left the room, hurrying out of the building and making her way to a nearby bus stop where she sat down, the cool metal of the bench a sharp contrast to the heat in the air.

She covered her mouth and cried, allowing herself one brief moment of weakness, her father's words cutting her deeper than his weapon ever could. She heard footsteps approaching from behind her, so she wiped her tears away, sat up straight, and turned to see Navid, his face sorrowful and bewildered.

"Are you all right?" he asked, sitting next to her.

"I'm fine. I told you to go."

"There's no way I'm leaving now. Not after what I've just seen."

"What did you see?"

"I was watching through the window. I heard everything."

She looked around, checking for passersby. The street was quiet.

"You called that man 'Father', but he looks no older than you and he hasn't aged a day since I saw him murder my mother."

She looked at him, her features softening. "What?"

"He didn't know I was there. I was hiding, stuffed in a hamper. I was four years old, but I'll remember his face for the rest of my life. *It was him.* Wasn't it?"

"Probably, yes."

"And he wants to kill you, too? He called you a monster? Why?"

"Because I *am* a monster. Queen of monsters. I'm very sorry about what happened to your mother. I don't know why he would kill her. Just his nature, I suppose. You should go home. Forget you ever met me. Forget what you heard. *Forget* about my father." She stood to go, but he grabbed her wrist.

"You said we were related."

"It doesn't matter."

"You said distantly, but how distant can it be if you have my mother's eyes?"

She stopped, her heart leaping to her throat.

"My mother was my only living relative. I was adopted by strangers from another city. Who are you? Please, I need to know who you are so I can understand who *I* am."

"All right," she relented. "Where are you staying?"

Chapter 12

Wendy arrived at the lodge, exhausted after an eighteen-and-a-half-hour flight. There was a lovely patio with an umbrellaed table, a cozy living room, kitchenette, bathroom, and spacious bedroom where she dropped her bags, then herself, onto the queen-sized bed. Just as she was about to kick her shoes off and settle in for a nap, a knock came on the glass patio door. She groaned and got up to answer it, bumping into the dresser as she went, grunting, more agitated than hurt.

She recognized the older woman waving excitedly as she slid the door open to let her in as the witch that had called her here, begging for help.

"Wendy!" she chirped, giving her a quick hug. "So glad you're here. How was your flight?"

"Long," she said, flashing her a smile.

"Right," she laughed, her accent so endearing that Wendy's annoyance drifted away. "Well, I'm Charlotte. Sorry to bug you already, but this is pretty time-sensitive."

"I understand. Let's sit." They took a seat on the blue, leather sofa. "So, what exactly are we dealing with?"

"You know the legend of Maui?"

"Just the cartoon version."

She held back a snicker. "Well, the myths deviate quite substantially from his actual history."

"Why doesn't that surprise me?"

"Maui was a warlock, born into a family who controlled very strong magic. As a child, his grandmother told him stories about an island that sank to the bottom of the ocean many generations before. She told him about the beautiful beaches and interesting wildlife. She spoke of waterfalls and mountains and sunsets so spectacular, they were like something from a dream. His brothers told him it was a fairy tale, but he so loved it that he was determined to make it real. When his grandmother died, he used her jawbone, his blood, and a karakia to work a spell. Now, no one knows for sure if he created the island or just pulled it up from the depths, but either way, it's now called 'Te Ika-a-Maui', or 'The North Island'."

"Where we are now."

"Yes, exactly. Seems well enough, right? But, as Maui got older, he became obsessed with ruling over his island. He loved it so much, he never wanted to leave it. Like, *never*. So, he sought out a powerful witch who was said to know the secrets of immortality named Hine-nui-te-po. She lived deep in a cave, in hiding from her handsy father. He wooed her with gifts of exotic birds whose songs were the most beautiful she'd ever heard. He bottled the rays of the sun, giving her light where she'd never had any. He made her happy for maybe the first time in her life. He tricked her into falling in love with him, thinking that she would share her secret spells. One night, when they were...*together*, she noticed one of the birds, a fantail. Unbeknownst to Maui, one of her powers was animal communication. The bird was nervous, so she went into its mind and saw its memories, memories of Maui making plans to deceive her. She was livid, so she took a dagger made of obsidian and jammed it into his back."

"While he was still," She made an awkward thrusting motion.

Charlotte nodded, eyebrows raised. "She stuck him a few times, actually, until he stopped moving. When she was sure he was dead, she vowed that one day, she'd be reborn and she'd take her revenge again, this time by plunging his precious island back into the sea. Then, she worked a spell using his blood, the blood of the bird, and her own. For the spell to work and bring her back, she had to sacrifice her life, so she slit her throat."

"Holy crap balls. So, you need me because you think she's back?"

"We're fairly sure. There have been a lot of earthquakes lately, geysers are more active. Almost four million people live here now. It's the perfect time for her to return if her goal is to inflict as much damage as possible. My coven and I are little more than holistic medicine peddlers. We're no match for someone like her. But a Tituban witch might stand a fighting chance."

Wendy chewed the inside of her cheek as she pondered, her mind so fatigued, it was hard to string a coherent thought together. "Okay, I'm having some serious brain fog right now, so let me get a few hours of sleep and meet me back here with the coven in the morning."

"Oh, of course. Get some sleep. The girls and I will see you bright and early."

Wendy had just pulled on her sweater when she heard chattering coming from the living room. When she got there, she found twelve women, talking and seeming to be in good spirits, sitting around the coffee table.

"Wendy!" Charlotte greeted, breaking away from the group. "Come, sit. We've brought meat pies and L&P. Alice makes *the best* pies."

A woman, presumably Alice, waved from the sofa. Wendy smiled and took a seat next to her, picking up a pie from the table and taking a bite. Her eyes widened and she nodded. "She *does* make the best pies."

"Why, thank you, dear," the woman, who had to be in her late seventies, said. "I'll be sure to get you the recipe."

"Thank you." She tried to sense the magic in the room, but only a tiny bit sparked from Charlotte. Everyone else here was almost void of it entirely. *This isn't a coven*, she thought. *It's a goddamn book club.* "So, do you ladies know where we might find the resurrected witch we're after?"

The room went quiet, all of the women turning their eyes to Charlotte, whose expression went from chipper to defeated. She took a deep breath and folded her hands in her lap, appearing to be afraid of how Wendy would respond to what she had to say. She looked her in the eye, took another breath, and answered, "We have no idea."

"All right. I'll walk around the island, see if I can sense her."

"Just like that?" Charlotte exchanged dumbfounded glances with some of the other women. "You can just...*feel* her?"

"I can feel *magic* and if she's as strong as you say she is, it won't be hard to point her out in a crowd." She took another bite of pie. "*God*, these really are *good*."

"It's the garlic," Alice said proudly. "I add a little extra."

"Hmm."

"You can *feel magic*?" Charlotte asked, visibly stunned.

"Yeah, I'm a witch. So, I'm gonna walk around, see what I can see. Who knows? Maybe what's going on with the island is completely natural."

The women exchanged knowing glances which made Wendy think of the phrases, 'Oh, girl' and 'Bless her heart'. She ignored it and took a sip of soda as she stood to go. "Stay here, make yourselves comfortable. I'll be back when I know something. Hey, can I take another one of these pies with me?"

Alice grinned from ear to ear. "Of course, dear."

"Thanks." She took a pie, her soda, and a napkin and headed out, half expecting to find nothing at all.

Chapter 13

Michelle tossed an empty blood bag on the pile on the coffee table. Her leg was nearly vibrating, she was tapping her foot so fast. No one had come by asking about the man in the truck and she wasn't sure if she should be relieved or if it had just not occurred to the police to interrogate her…yet. She gathered up her trash and shoved it down into the can in the kitchen before washing her hands. She paced the room, memories of finding Will on the floor, bleeding and covered in wolf bites clawing at her mind. Tears filled her eyes as her hands began to shake. It was all she could do to keep herself from going up to his room, throwing herself on his bed, and never getting up again. She wanted to exist there, desiccating in her own misery until even the hunger left her. She could go up there right now, lay down, and let herself die.

She shook her head, pushing the thought from her mind and sitting at the dining table. She held her hands together and tapped them on her forehead as she tried to get herself together. In the distance, she could hear a wolf howl and her despair turned to rage. "Don't do it," she told herself. "Stay your ass here. Do not leave this house." She put her head down and gripped the sides of her chair, trembling, physically holding herself back from the pain she wanted to inflict. He'd told her that he'd killed the entire pack that attacked him, but had he? Or were there more, haunting the woods like ghosts, waiting for Will to come back. But he wasn't coming back. He would never come back. He was lost to her. Forever.

She reached a shaky hand into her back pocket and pulled out her phone. She called Gabriel first, but there was no answer, so she dialed Hattie's number, a burner to be used only in case of an emergency.

"Michelle? What's wrong?" she answered.

"I'm not okay. I need help."

"Have you met with Gabriel?"

"Yeah, she took Sinclair. She's sending me blood bags, but I'm going through them too fast. I'm always hungry and *I'm so mad*. Jesus Christ, Hattie, I'm so mad all the time. I go from wanting to die to wanting to go on a murder binge."

"I'm so sorry, dear, but I told you this would happen. You should have stayed with me. I could have helped you."

"You wanted me to kill my baby."

"Yes, before the Queen did, when she was older and aware of her circumstances."

"Gabriel can protect her."

"Are you sure about that? I've seen the Queen do things that would curl your hair."

"My hair's already curly and if it's a smackdown between the vampire Queen and God's Messenger, I'm putting my money on the angel every time."

"Yes, fine. So, what do you need from me?"

"Can I come back to stay with you in Scotland? I know it's risky, but--"

"Risky's an understatement, but it doesn't matter. I was just packing my things to leave this place. I'm fairly certain Her Majesty's spies are closing in on me here. Text me your address and I'll come to you."

Allydia sat across from her descendant at the round dining table in the tiny apartment he was renting for the week. It smelled of stale cigarettes and shattered dreams. Whoever owned this place was a sad individual, indeed.

"My name is Allydia Cain," she began, noting how interested he seemed to be as she spoke, like he was starving for words. "I'm a vampire."

He laughed out loud. "A what?"

"Vampire. Queen of vampires, actually. I'm the first."

"You're joking."

"Something you should know about me," She opened her mouth and bared her fangs. He jumped back in his seat and she returned her teeth to their normal size. "I don't lie."

"What the," His voice trailed off as he stared.

"Before I was turned, I had three daughters. They went on to have children of their own who had children and so on for thousands of years. Lines died out over time and now *you* are the last of my descendants. Well, there is one other, an old Greek woman, but after the fright my father gave her, I may leave her be."

His face was blank, his mouth hanging open.

"My father is Cain, son of Adam. He doesn't age because he's been cursed by God. How familiar are you with religious literature?"

"Cain? As in, Cain and Abel?"

"Yes, that's right. He's everything you think he is and worse. As for me, I'm no danger to you. But, if the others find out who you are, you wouldn't be safe. That's why I told you to leave. Humans are little more than playthings and food to most of my people. They will not hesitate to use you in any way they can if they don't just kill you outright. That's why you must go. Do you understand?"

"But, Cain--"

"Has no clue you exist. As long as he doesn't see us together, you'll be fine."

He entwined his fingers as if in prayer and rested his chin on his hands, his eyes locked on hers. "Let me tell you a story, mm?"

"All right."

"Me mum grew up in Ahvaz. She had a good life. Family, friends. She grew up, got a good job. She was happy. When she was twenty, both her parents died in a plane crash. They were going on holiday for their anniversary. She was crushed. She decided to go on holiday herself. Took a trip to Italy where she had wine for the first time. She got wasted, completely sloshed, every night for a week. Her last night there, she did it up proper. Club hoppin', pub crawl, the whole thing. At one of them pubs, she met a man. He started chattin' her up, tellin' her she was tidy, she looked exotic. Said he fancied her, right? So, he followed her 'round the whole night like a dog on a leash and me mum got smitten. Took him back to her hotel and you can guess where that went, yeah? Next day, he's gone. No note, nothin'. She didn't even know his name. So, she went home, didn't think of it again. Then, the country's invaded. There's a war on. In the midst of that, she realized she hadn't gotten her monthly. So she fled. Took the last of her money and went to London where she had me. Life was hard, her bein' illegal, but we had a roof over our heads and food in our bellies, and on my life, I *never* heard that woman complain. She was amazin' and I loved her. Then, one day, I'm watchin' telly and there's a knock on the door. She looked out the spyhole and saw a bloke she didn't recognize. Thought he might be immigration enforcement, so she hid me in a hamper and told me to stay quiet. Through the openings in the wicker, I could see her let him in. I couldn't hear what was bein' said, but everything seemed fine for a while, til she got this look on her face. Same look she gave me when I fell off the back of the sofa and got a lump on my head. Terror mixed with fury. I saw her waving him toward the door, but he wouldn't leave. I watched him slap her across the face and I stayed hidden while he took an iron spike out of a briefcase and plunge it into her heart like it was his fuckin' job. Like he couldn't care less. He killed my mother. I can't leave without bringing him to justice."

"I understand," she told him. "He kidnapped three of my daughters and offered up the fourth to my stepmother as a sacrifice to make me what I am. He's a monster, maybe more so than I am. But, there is no justice for someone as cruel as my father. At least, not that can be administered by human hands."

"So, I should let it go, is what you're sayin'? How? And what about you?"

"What about me?"

"You're my ancestor, yeah? The only family I have left in the world besides that evil son of a bitch. You're tellin' me I can't get to know ya? And I should also just ignore the fact that vampires are real creatures walkin' amongst us. How in the world am I supposed to do that?"

"You do it by going home, going to work, visiting with friends. You find someone to love and build a life with them. Have children. Create the family you've always wanted and that you deserve. You live your life and be grateful that you have it." She stood. "Go home, Navid. Be happy." She left, finally allowing the tears she'd been fighting to fall down her cheeks. She wept as she walked, wishing there was a way for her to have Navid in her life. But, there wasn't. Her existence put him in danger and as much as it pained her, he was better off without her.

Wyatt woke to the soft touch of Allydia's fingertips on his cheek. "You're back," he said, his voice scratchy as he lifted his head. "How was your trip? How are your, what, great-great, a hundred times great-grandkids?" He turned on the light and saw the tears streaming down her face. "What happened?" He scooted closer to her as she sat.

"My father hates me and I just had to tell my perfect, beautiful, amazing however-many-times grandson that he can never see me again because doing so could put his life in danger."

He wiped the tears from her cheeks and tucked her hair behind her ears. "I'm sorry. Is there anything I can do?"

"You can tell me what my father was doing here. Did he hurt you?"

"Hurt me? No."

"What, then?"

"It doesn't matter."

"Wyatt,"

"He's a dick. He gave me a bullshit speech, trying to defend himself. He thinks he did the right thing, taking your kids away. He thinks you're dangerous. He warned me that I should," He looked into her eyes, her heartbreak giving him pause. "It's not important."

"He warned you about what? Me?"

He took a sip of water from the bottle on the nightstand and put it back.

"He warned you about me. He said I would hurt you?"

"He said he thinks you'll kill me."

"That's absurd. You can't die."

"That's what I said."

She swallowed the lump in her throat as she held back more tears. "He told you to leave me."

"I told you, it doesn't matter."

She studied his face, looking for signs of deception. There weren't any.

"He's twisted. Resentful. Mad at God and everyone else, it seems like. He doesn't know what he's talking about. Besides, you think I'm gonna take relationship advice from someone that married *Lilith*?"

They both laughed.

"I *am* dangerous, though. I'd like to say, 'not to you' because I would never want to harm you, but when I found you in the bath and you yelled at me to leave and you hurt yourself..."

He touched her cheek, the guilt rising in his chest like stomach acid.

"The sight of your blood, the aroma of it, it did things to me. Things I'm not proud to admit."

"And you left. I know that you left so you wouldn't hurt me. I'm not worried about you attacking me. At all."

She nodded, a single tear falling from her eye.

"I'm here," he told her. "I'm right here and I'm not going anywhere."

More tears fell as she covered her mouth.

"What's wrong?"

"Navid," she whimpered. "That's his name. He said I have his mother's eyes. His mother, who my father killed in front of him when he was a child. He has no family but me. He's alone."

Wyatt pulled her into his chest and held her, kissing her head as she cried. "I'm sorry." He kissed her again. "I'm so sorry."

"I'd rather not discuss it further. Can we just sleep?"

"Yeah," he said, leaning back, positioning her in the crook of his arm. "Yeah, let's sleep."

Chapter 14

Malik bounced Sinclair in his arms as he rocked her, quietly singing "In My Life" as she howled, her tears soaking through his tee-shirt.

"I thought Gabriel said she liked Beatles songs!" he called to Valerie, who was in the nursery, busy putting a clean sheet on the crib mattress.

"She does!"

He sighed and went back to singing, but the baby continued to cry, kicking her legs and smacking her hand against his chest. After a few minutes, Malik gave up, carrying the hysterical child into her mother. "I've tried everything. She's been changed, fed, played with, and sang to. She's freaking out like she's scared of something."

"Give her to me," Valerie said, holding her hands out. She took a turn rocking her, rubbing her back, and humming the tune to "Let It Be". Sinclair continued to wail, pulling her mother's hair and beating her tiny fist against her shoulder. "Somebody's in a mood. What's your problem, Miss Perry? Do you have a tooth coming in?" She poked her finger in the child's mouth but felt no new protrusions.

"You think a bath would help? We could break out that lavender soap your sister brought over."

"I think she's just tired." She went back to humming, sitting in the rocking chair, and closing the blinds, dimming the room. After a few moments, the baby began to drift off, her cries now barely whimpers. Soon, she was quiet and relief washed over the exhausted parents.

Suddenly, a knock came on the front door. "You get it," Valerie ordered. "I am *not* moving. I don't care if it's a camera crew with a comically giant check, I'm not getting up *for shit*."

He laughed and backed out of the room, gently pulling the door closed behind him. The knocking turned to pounding as Malik walked back to the living room. Before he could answer, the door burst open, the man on the other side having kicked it in.

"The fuck?" Malik boomed.

Cain swung his briefcase, landing it squarely into Malik's jaw. He fell back, but quickly recovered, leaping to his feet and planting himself between the man and the hallway leading to the bedrooms. "You're messing with the wrong motherfucker."

"Am I? I believe you're exactly who I'm here for." He swiftly took the spike from the case and held it over his head, rushing toward the new father, causing him to change his position, dodging the weapon while wildly glancing around the room for one of his own.

Valerie emerged from the nursery, her brows furrowed in annoyance. "What in the holy fuck is going on--" She stopped, taking notice of the strange man in her apartment and the mess of what used to be her front door. "Who the fuck are you?"

"You must be Uriel," Cain huffed. "I thought you'd be at school. No matter. I'm almost done here. Just need to impale your human, then I'll be on my way."

In the distance, Sinclair again began to scream.

Cain's eyes lit up. "You have a child, angel? *Delicious*. I'll take them from you, as well." But as he took a step toward her, he was knocked to the ground by a cast iron pan to the back of the head. Malik stood over him, out of breath and sweating.

"Any ideas?"

Valerie shook her head and they both shrugged before heading back to the nursery and gathering up their crying daughter.

"Should we call the cops?" Malik packed the diaper bag while Valerie put Sinclair in her car seat.

"Nah, this is some 'other' shit. He knew who I was. Best take this mess straight to my sister.

Lucifer entered Mariana's apartment, yanking down the police tape that hung in front of the door. His heart pounded like a drum in his chest, the sound of his own blood pumping in his ears the only thing he could hear. He stepped slowly through the living room and down the hall, dreading what he'd find once he came to the bedroom, its door also taped off. He pulled it down and went inside, the sight of blood and the outline of a body on the carpet causing the veins in his neck to throb. All of the times he'd had to track down demons on Earth and in all the years he'd spent in Hell, nothing had ever made him as angry as he was in that moment. *Nothing.*

As he turned to leave, he noticed the writing on the mirror, letters written in blood that spelled out the word, *Akrotiri.*

"The fuck, bitch?" Valerie shouted as she let herself into the apartment.

Gabriel sighed, getting up from her spot at the island and putting her danish down on her plate. "It's Cain. I didn't think he'd go after *you*, Holy Fire, and everything. Something must've pissed him off *extra*." She took Sinclair out of her seat and kissed her cheek. "Hey, pretty girl." The baby giggled and grabbed her finger. "Check the junk drawer for keys."

Valerie opened the kitchen drawer and rifled through unopened mail, bits of paper with what looked like shopping lists written on them, a stapler, three double-A batteries, and a dead glow stick before finding a pair of keys on a ring. "What are these to?"

"Your house. Well, my old house, but yours now. You're welcome!"

"Girl,"

"The house I grew up in. I just had it remodeled. Four bedrooms, three and a half baths, huge chef's kitchen. Take it. You'll be safe there."

"I'm not letting you buy me a house."

"I didn't buy it, I inherited it, and I have zero interest in moving back in. If you don't take it, I'll just sell it and it's not like I need the money."

Valerie folded her arms and bit her lip as she thought it over.

"Come on," Gabriel prodded. "Sinclair wants to go. Look how happy she is." The baby flashed a toothless grin and squawked in agreement.

"Fine," she reluctantly agreed, putting the child back in her seat. "Where is it?"

Gabriel picked up her phone and began typing. "Texting the address now."

Malik rubbed his temple. "You'll have to drive. I've got a migraine."

Valerie took the car keys and checked her phone, shooting Gabriel an irritated glare. "Bitch, what am I gonna do in *Connecticut*?"

She sat back down and took a bite of danish. Still chewing, she replied, "Keep your family alive."

Chapter 15

Wendy wandered around a busy shopping district in the town of Hamilton. There were people pushing strollers, riding bikes, talking on cell phones. There were buses and park benches, bars and restaurants. It all looked very normal. But as she got closer to the Waikato River, she began to sense it: the dark energy that filled the air like cigarette smoke in an otherwise sterile room. She dipped a hand into the water and was immediately bombarded by the dark magic. It was stronger than any she'd felt in the past and it was not human in origin. "What did you do?" she whispered to the long-dead witch that now threatened the island.

She spent hours searching, combing through the most remote places, hoping against hope that she was wrong, but she wasn't. She knew it in her bones. The witch hadn't been reincarnated as a human being. She'd come back as something else. Something dark. A vengeful spirit, her hate filling everything on the island. Every blade of grass, every grain of sand. It was all tainted. Soon, the people would become infected, turning on one another like rabid animals, *if* the island's structural integrity held out that long. It was pulling itself apart, she could tell by the fear she saw in the animals as they passed. From dogs tugging on leashes to birds screeching across the sky, they were all terrified. As she made her way back to town for supplies, the ground rumbled beneath her, throwing her to her knees and sending a flock of robins soaring from the trees and fluttering off into the distance. Time was running out. She had to act fast. Millions of lives depended on it.

"You were right," she said as she reentered the lodge, getting the attention of the coven who had been busy placing protection idols around the rooms, burning sage, and putting together protective hex bags for themselves and Wendy. She set her bags on the floor and put her hands on her hips. "I thought maybe there was nothing weird going on. I was dumb."

"So, you found her?" Charlotte asked, handing her a hex bag, hope filling her eyes.

"Oh, I found that crazy bitch, all right."

"Did you," another woman asked sheepishly. "You know, take care of it?"

"No. I can't handle this on my own. I mean, I probably could, with enough time, but there isn't any. She's tearing the island up. It'll be underwater in a few days if we don't stop her. This thing can't be reasoned with or bound."

"Well, dear," Alice chimed in. "We don't want you to *reason* with her. We want you to *kill* her."

"I'm afraid I can't do that, either. Not that I would. What kind of person do you think I am?"

"Excuse my language, dear, but why the hell not?"

"I'm not a murderer, Alice. Jesus. Savage much?"

"But, you know where she is?" Charlotte asked.

"Yeah. Bitch is everywhere. She's not human. She brought herself back as an angry Earth Spirit. Like I said, she can't be killed. I can't bind her magic, she's got no corporeal form, nothing I can make an effigy of. There's only one thing we can do and I'll need all of your help to get it done. We have to banish her."

"How do we do that?"

She picked up the shopping bags and grinned. "I bought supplies. I hope you're all well-hydrated."

Chapter 16

The women worked tirelessly, writing the ancient witch's name on three by three paper bags, wrapping them around walnuts, and tying them with black yarn. They then dropped their bundles in bottles filled with their own urine.

"Is the urine really necessary?" One of the women asked, holding her nose.

"Yeah," Wendy told her. "We could have used vinegar, but this is way more effective. I don't know about you ladies, but I don't want to take *any* chances."

"Is it okay if I'm scared?" one of the women asked.

"Sure. It's normal to be scared. We're going up against some powerful stuff. I'd be worried about you if you *weren't* scared."

"I just really wish you didn't need our help. We're not exactly...like you. Sorry, that was rude."

"It's fine. Listen, I wish I could've just handled this on my own, too. If she was a *person*, I'd take a picture of her, print it out, a five-minute binding spell," she rubbed her hands together. "All over. But this thing is everywhere. I need you guys. I know it's a lot, but I promise, you'll be fine."

"Are you entirely sure about that?" Charlotte asked, screwing the top on one of the bottles.

"Ninety percent." She winked.

"And the other ten?"

"My grandma always told me never to get cocky when it comes to magic. All done?"

The women nodded, placing the last of the bottles in the box. Wendy picked it up and shuffled out the door. "Load up! We've got a pissed off Earth Spirit to banish."

The women scattered across the island, each digging holes and burying their bottles at designated locations: the cities of Wellington, Napier, Gisborne, New Plymoth,

Rotorua, Tauranga, Aukland, Wangarei, Paihia, Kaitaia, and beaches along the eastern shore, effectively encircling the entirety of the island. It was getting late when they met up on the shore of Lake Taupo, a caldera of the Taupo Volcano, the center of the island.

"You ladies ready?" Wendy asked, seeing in their faces that they weren't. They were terrified and with good reason. As they'd been working, the earthquakes had become more frequent, growing in intensity as the hours passed. Hine-nui-te-po knew what they were up to and she was displeased.

Charlotte fiddled with the hex bag that hung around her neck. "I think I can speak for everyone here when I say that we're nervous as shit, but we're ready to fight."

The women all nodded in agreement, some rubbing their arms for warmth, others checking to make sure their own hex bags were still in place. Wendy waved her hands toward herself, gathering them closer. "Everything will be fine. Half of magic is setting a clear intention. So, come on. Everyone hold hands in a circle, close your eyes, and picture a giant wave of bright, white light, pushing away the dark energy in the island." The women complied, joining hands, and forming a perfect circle. Wendy squeezed in, taking Charlotte's hand with her left and Alice's with her right. As she closed her eyes, the ground shook beneath them, threatening to knock them down. "Don't break the circle. Whatever you do, *do not let go.*"

Birds screeched across the sky above them as Wendy began to chant, "Whakakahoretia te kino", a Maori Karakia meaning simply, 'Get rid of evil'. The ladies joined in, repeating the phrase over and over as the sky went dark. The Earth shook violently, but the women continued, bending their knees as if they were riding a wave, all keeping their eyes shut tight for fear of what they might see. All, except for Wendy.

She stared sternly into the dense cloud of smoke that rose from the volcano as she chanted, doing her best to ignore the lava that had begun to flow down its sides. Slowly, what looked like a woman's face began to appear in the black plume. Its eyes were angry, nostrils flared, and its mouth was opened so wide, it looked like a caricature. From the billowing darkness came a piercing scream, filling the air and rustling the leaves of the trees behind them. Wendy felt Alice losing her grip, so she squeezed tighter, never taking her eyes off of the spirit.

After ninety or so seconds that felt like an eternity, the shrieking stopped. The ground went still and the smoke subsided, dissipating in the starry night sky. The women went quiet, ending their chanting, and opening their eyes.

"Is that it?" one of them wondered.

"Yep," Wendy told them, letting go of her new friends' hands and taking a deep breath, letting it out with an audible, "Ah."

"It's over?" Charlotte asked. "Just like that?"

"Just like that. She won't be back."

"But, how can you be sure?"

"This isn't my first rodeo."

After a moment of stunned silence, the women cheered, throwing up their arms and dancing in the sand.

"We have to celebrate!" Charlotte proclaimed. "Everyone, meet back at the hotel. I'll bring the booze. Party at Wendy's!"

Back at the lodge, the women drank beer and danced around the living room while listening to Split Enz on one of the ladies' phones. Wendy sat back on the sofa, smiling as she watched them. She took a sip of her drink and leaned her head back, barely able to keep her eyes open.

"Tired, dear?" Alice asked, sitting next to her.

"Yeah," she admitted. "It's good, though. My flight home leaves soon. I might just be able to sleep the whole way."

"Well, that's nice. Before I forget," she patted her knee and reached into her pocket. "Here's that pie recipe."

"Thank you, Alice."

"You're welcome, dear. I'm going to get another beer before Charlotte drinks them all. Such a lush."

Wendy laughed. "I didn't have you pegged for that big of a drinker."

"Oh, yes. I may need help getting up from the couch, but I can still drink these girls under the table. I'm old, not dead."

She laughed again, setting her drink on the end table and helping the older woman stand. As the women drunkenly attempted to sing along to "I See Red", all of them off-key and slurring their words, Wendy shook her head and muttered under her breath, "Not *just* a book club."

Chapter 17

Libby rocked back and forth in her porch swing, eyes closed, breathing in the balmy summer air. It would be her last summer, she knew, and she wanted to savor every bit of it.

"Quassatura," she heard as a sharp pain spread across her cheek. She held her hand to it, the blood appearing on her fingers causing her blood pressure to rise.

"What insolence is this?" the old woman hissed, grasping her cane as she stood. At the bottom of the porch steps, three women appeared, members of her own coven, their looks of determination fueling her anger.

"Sorry, Libby," Julia said. "I was just checking."

"Checking what?"

"If you had Grace's magic, you know, in you."

"What have you been smoking, child? If I had Grace's magic, I would have shared it with the rest of you. You know that."

The women climbed the steps, Julia in the lead. "I don't know anything except that without the Tituban magic, we're powerless against the other covens. I know you think I'm being paranoid, but--"

"Paranoid and treasonous!" Libby barked. "You *do not* attack one of your sisters, especially an elder. I should have you shunned."

"But, you can't because you're not our leader. We have no leader. And until Grace's magic is found, we're all but helpless. Now, if you don't mind, I'm just gonna come in and do a little search. See if you and our departed founder were in cahoots."

"Redipiscor!" Libby ordered, holding her hand out in front of her. The witches flew back, off the porch and onto the ground.

"I don't want to hurt you, old woman, but I will have that magic," Julia said through her teeth.

"Is that what this is about? You want Grace's power for yourself? *You* want to lead the coven?" Libby cackled. "*You?* You don't have the temperament, clearly, or the discipline. You're far too emotional, which is why half of your spells don't work the way you intend. If you took in *an ounce* of Grace's magic, it would burn you alive from the inside. Get off my property while I call the other elders so we can decide what to do about you." She went inside and picked up her phone, trying to remember how to do a group text. "Damn technology," she muttered. As she hit send, a cold chill went up her spine. She could feel the floor beneath her begin to rumble. Soon, the glass in the windows began to shake, pictures fell from walls, and lights flickered. The door flew open, the three witches storming in.

"I didn't want to do it this way," Julia said. "But if that magic's here, I *will* find it."

"Oh, sweetie, you have no idea who you're messing with. Ventus." The three were blown back in a gust of wind, pinned to the wall, the air moving so fast, they could hardly breathe. Libby ran from the room, dialing Poe's number as she hustled to her bedroom.

"Libby?" Poe answered.

"Yes, child, it's me. Listen, Julia, Sonya, and Hallie are here looking for Grace's magic. I know you don't have it, but I suspect you know where it is. I don't want you to tell me, I know Grace had her reasons for keeping it from us. Her magic, her decision. But, these girls are on a mission. Julia wants the power for herself and she'll do anything to get it. Under no circumstances can she be allowed to get her hands on it, do you hear me?"

"Yes, ma'am."

"I want you to run, child. Take only what you need and go, tonight. When she figures out none of us old broads has what she's after, she'll no doubt come after you."

"Okay. I'll take off. Thanks, Libby."

She ended the call and braced herself as the bedroom door flew open. "Where is it, Libby?" Julia snapped.

She locked her fingers around the cane. "I don't have it, and if I did, I certainly wouldn't give it to you."

"Obfoco!"

Libby held her hand to her throat as she began to choke. The three searched the room as she struggled to breathe, tossing the contents of her drawers onto the bed and pawing through her closet. Libby could feel herself growing weak, her peripheral vision filling with stars. With all of her energy, she lifted the cane and took a swing, landing a sharp blow to the back of Julia's knee. She buckled, her spell broken.

"Definitely treason." Libby whacked her again, this time in the shin, then the stomach. She turned her attention to the other two, swatting them both in the diaphragm, knocking the air out of them. She hit Julia once more, slamming the cane across her face before leaving the room in a mad dash for the front door. But as she rushed, she heard the fatal word being called out from behind.

"Ictum!"

She was stopped in her tracks by the unbelievable pain, like a bullet to the head. Her entire left side went numb as her cane fell to the floor. Her left eye closed, then the other. She collapsed, Sonya and Hallie looking on in shock as Julia stood over her. She bent down, able to feel the old woman's magic dissipate. She was dead.

"Check her phone," Julia ordered. "I want to know who she was talking to in there."

"This charm will protect you," Poe told the bunny as she placed the collar back around its neck. "Hold still. I won't hurt you." She picked up the scissors from the table and snipped a bit of fur from the rabbit's back, adding it to the mortar. She used the pestle to combine the hairs into the mixture and used a syringe to feed some to Raven before dipping her finger in and licking it. "Assuesco. Come on, let's pack." She ran through the house, throwing spellbooks and clothes in a backpack before picking the bunny up and placing her gently inside. She zipped it most of the way, leaving a pocket open so Raven could breathe, and headed for the door.

"Where are you off to?" she heard Julia ask. She turned, facing the three witches for the second time. "I know Libby called you. Warned you. She thinks you know where Grace's magic is. But you told me that's not true, right? And you wouldn't lie, would you, Poe?"

"I don't have it."

"I didn't ask if you had it. I know that you don't. I'm just wondering why you would keep it from us. We're sisters, aren't we?"

"You know, I thought so, but then you broke in my place and put a gash in my arm, so you'll have to forgive me if I'm not feeling the whole 'coven buddy' thing right now."

"Come on, Poe. Sweet, androgynous, summer child Poe. You can't fight us. Hand it over and we can all be friends again. I swear. No hard feelings."

"I don't--"

"Tell me where it is!"

She cocked her head and pursed her lips. "I wouldn't tell you where Grace hid her magic if my life depended on it."

"Are you sure? Because it literally does. Demeo."

Poe fell, dropping her pack.

"I won't ask again."

"Silentium!" She shot back, taking the witches' voices. Julia looked genuinely surprised that the younger witch had the power to pull off the spell as she tried to speak. Poe grabbed her backpack and leaped up, but Sonya threw her back to the ground. She and Hallie kicked her in the ribs and spine while Julia silently laughed.

With the pack lying on the floor, Raven slipped out, making a beeline for the witches. First, the bunny hopped up onto Sonya's shoulder and clamped down on the side of her neck, tearing out tissue as blood squirted from the wound. Hallie mouthed the words, "what the fuck" as the rabbit came for her next, running at her so fast, she couldn't see it anymore. *Where'd it go*? she thought, confused by the horrified stares on Julia and Poe's faces. She turned around and there it was, its fur soaked with so much blood, it dripped from its floppy ears. Julia had gone stark white, her mouth hanging open as she pointed. Finally, Hallie looked down and saw it, the gaping hole in her abdomen. The rabbit had run straight through her. She fell, dead before she hit the floor.

Poe gathered her senses and opened the pack. "Tersus," she said, the blood disappearing from Raven's fur. The bunny hopped into the bag and Poe zipped it most of the way. "Maneat!" She bolted from the house, Julia being rendered immobile for the moment and unable to follow her. The spell wouldn't last long, so she needed to hurry. There was only one place still safe, but for how long? It was only a matter of time before Julia found Wendy. She *had* to warn her.

Chapter 18

Lucifer was seething when he got to Gabriel's apartment. She set her soda can down on the kitchen counter as he approached her, the look in his eyes worrying her.

"Where is he?" he snarled.

"God, I'm so sorry. I didn't know--"

"Where?!"

She pleaded with her eyes. "He just attacked Malik. He's probably still there, but Lucifer--"

"I know the risks." He turned to go.

"Wait," she called after him, taking something from a small box on the counter and handing it to him. "Slip this in his pocket or something."

He looked at her, understanding mingling with the rage in his eyes. "Father's plan?"

Her voice cracked as she answered, "Yes."

He pursed his lips and nodded, slamming the door as he left. She slumped to the floor, pulling her legs into her chest and covering her mouth as tears slid down her cheeks, the sound of her own muffled sobs making her feel even worse. She put her head down on her knees, wishing she could wallow. But there was work to do. There was *always* work to do.

Valerie's neighbor stood outside the apartment, dialing nine-one-one as she peeked her head in to see the man lying on the floor. As he began to stir, the operator answered, "Nine-one-one, what's your emergency?"

"Hi, I think someone broke into my neighbor's--"

Lucifer snatched the phone from the woman's hand and crushed it in his, staring her down as her mouth fell open, her lip quivering in fear. "*Run away.*" She made the sign of the cross and did as he commanded, running so quickly down the stairs that she almost fell.

Cain got to his feet, placing a hand on the back of his head and then checking it for blood. There was none. "You got my message." He laughed as he leaned on the bar.

"Wouldn't want to be interrupted." Lucifer hoisted the door up to cover the entrance. "Tell me, son of Adam. Did you forget who I am or are you just breathtakingly stupid?"

"I know exactly who you are. You and the other angels in your self-righteous show of force vaporized my last chance at--" He stopped, sitting on a stool and waving his hand. "It doesn't matter. It's over. I am forever alone. So scold me as you wish. Scream, throw things. It makes no difference. As long as you and I remain on Earth, I will continue to take everything you hold dear. I will kill everyone that means anything to you. Probably best to remain untangled. You wouldn't want to feel this grief again, would you?"

"You've gone mad." Lucifer stepped toward him. "Do you honestly think that's what I'm here for? A tantrum?"

Cain's expression turned from mockery to confused concern. "You wouldn't dare hurt me. You know the consequences."

He grasped him by the collar, lifted him from the stool, and slammed him to the floor, the terror in his eyes spurring him on. He held Cain's throat in his hand and leaned in, all but whispering, "Consequences be damned."

He punched him, first in the jaw, then in the eye. He broke his nose, cheek, and brow bones. When he got bored of that, he picked him up and heaved him across the room, sending him flailing into a window, cracking the glass.

"Stop this now!" Cain pleaded. "You know what will happen!"

"Save your breath." He kicked him in the groin and threw him over his shoulder. "The air is thin where we're going." He broke out the remaining glass and took off out the window rocketing to the clouds, Cain screaming as he clung to Lucifer's shirt.

"What are you doing?!"

Once above the clouds, they hovered in place, Lucifer tossing him forward and holding him up by the neck. "I want you to know, I'll have no regrets. I will enjoy this and the memory of it for all eternity." He plunged his fist into Cain's abdomen, ripping out organ after organ and discarding them, letting them fall haphazardly to the Earth. Cain seized, blood pouring from his mouth, his eyes starting to glaze over. Lucifer reached into his pocket, taking the device Gabriel had given him and shoving it into his adversary's mouth, forcing it closed until he swallowed. "My Father sends His regards." And with that, he let go, dropping Cain twenty-thousand feet to the pavement waiting below. When he could no longer hear his screams, he flew off, heading back toward his sister's apartment. Once there, he staggered to his bedroom, closed the door, and crashed onto the mattress.

Camael sat on what passed for a bed, leaning against the concrete wall of his cell, reading "Beyond Good and Evil" for the third time. The other inmates were loud but not louder than his sister's voice in his head. *Get the keys.*

What's up, G?

I know you have that guard's keys. It's time to use them. I'm parked across the street. Move your ass.

I told you--

I know why you're here. I've been filled in. You have a job to do. Now.

He closed his book and sat up, taking a deep breath, and preparing himself. He hadn't been sure that this day would ever come and now that it had, he wasn't sure he was ready for it.

Dude, be in your feelings after you're in the car.

Fine, I'm coming. He got up, retrieved the keys, and opened his cell. The other inmates went quiet as he crept past. He ignored their looks of shocked interest as he tried to sneak past the guards, but in quarters that tight, sneaking *anywhere* was impossible.

A guard turned and reached for his weapon. "What the--" But Cam knocked him unconscious before he could finish the sentence. He barrelled through guard after guard, punching some and simply pushing others to the ground. The alarm sounded, blaring as emergency lights flashed and the other men still locked in their own cells cheered.

Once out of his block, he tore steel doors from their hinges, making his way to the main entrance and out of the building. Bullets whizzed through the air, some lodging in his back and legs, but he barely noticed. He made it to the street and spotted Gabriel waving from her black sports car. She started it up as he hopped inside. She sped off, happy that it had occurred to her to cover her license plate before making the trip.

"So," he grinned. "Where to?"

Chapter 19

Hattie covered her fiery curls with a shawl and hurriedly took her bags from the trunk of the cab. Her eyes darted around the busy street, the lights from the airport across the way brightening the just-darkened sky above it so fully, it almost felt like day. The cab drove off and she stepped onto the road, anxious to get on a plane and out of her native land. It was no longer safe for her there and she knew it.

As she reached the sidewalk on the other side, a van with dark tinted windows screeched to a stop. Two men in black hoodies hopped out of the back and rushed her. She tried to run, but they were as fast as she was.

"Hey!" a man yelled. "Get away from her!"

"Stop!" another commanded.

"Someone call the police!" a woman begged.

The humans attempted to come to her aid but were swiftly knocked back by the goons. They tossed her into the van, got in themselves, and drove away, leaving the bystanders flummoxed, several of them already on their phones with the authorities.

The vampires chained her, wrapping her in iron links until she could no longer move her limbs. She struggled, but they were older and more powerful. It was inevitable. She was as good as dead.

Cain's eyes flew open, the sound of the splashing water to his left startling him awake. Had he landed a few inches over, he would have woken up at the bottom of the Hudson. He'd died hundreds of times over the centuries, and coming to underwater was his absolute least favorite way of realizing that he hadn't stayed dead. He got himself up, stepping out of the indention in the freshly cracked concrete. His clothes were torn and covered in blood, but he was no worse for the wear. He bent down to tie his shoe and began the long walk back to his hotel.

He unlocked the door and entered the room, his heart jumping and horror spreading across his face at the sight of the two people waiting for him inside.

"Wendy, Malik, *and* the bartender?" the woman asked. "Is there a stalker gene I don't know about?" He tried to back out of the room. "Uh, uh." She waved in its direction, causing it to slam shut behind him. She sat cross-legged on the desk while the man leered at him from a chair in the corner. He didn't know who *he* was, but he'd recognized Gabriel right away. After the beating he'd received from Lucifer, he was in no condition to grapple with God's Messenger.

"This is my brother, Cam. Camael. You might recognize him by his full name...The Wrath of God."

Cain's eyes grew wide as they fell on the man sitting silently, forearms on his thighs, hands folded, his expression cold and unchanged.

"How did you find me?"

"That thing Lucifer shoved down your gullet? Tracking device. Sends your location right to my phone. When you woke up from your tussle and started heading this way, it wasn't hard to figure out where you were going. This is the only hotel this far west."

"Tracking device? Hard to imagine angels needing the help of human technology to do God's will. Lucifer said God sent His regards. So, Messenger, does He want to tell me something? Is he angry with me? Or just disappointed?"

Gabriel continued, ignoring his questions. "I should have gotten him to you as soon as Dad told me to, but I put it off. I love my brother. I didn't want him to go. Had I known what you were up to, maybe I would've acted earlier. Maybe I wasn't supposed to act earlier. Who knows? Mysteries to be revealed at a later date, I guess."

"God's Wrath?"

"Totes. Only thing that can kill you permanently. See, God's salty that you basically wiped out your entire line. Seems you haven't learned your lesson and He's concerned that you'll find your last male heir and take him out before he procreates, which would be bad for some reason."

"My...there's another?"

"Oh, yeah. Allydia filled him in on your psychotic family history, put him on a plane back to where he came from. He'll be all right, eventually."

"And you've come to," He swallowed hard. "Kill me?"

"Don't get excited. You *will* die and you *will* go to Purgatory, but you'll never be reborn. You'll never set foot on this planet again."

"What do you mean? That's not possible. Elohim may be angry with me, but He *always* forgives."

"Yeah, but you're too much of a risk. Someday, when the human race goes extinct, God will welcome you home, you know," She pointed to the ceiling. "Up there. When He does, I hope you bring some knee pads, because you'll have some serious groveling to do. God will forgive you, but the souls of all the people you've killed, *your own relatives*, will need convincing."

"You're much more flippant than I remember."

"A lifetime of bullshit will do that to a girl."

"This is a lot of talking," Cam complained, sitting up straight. "Can I just kill this guy, already?"

"I'm just explaining to him why he's gotta die."

"You're stalling."

She rolled her eyes and crossed her arms.

"This is what I'm here for, G. I get it. It's all right."

Cain reached for the door, but it wouldn't budge. He scrambled to find a weapon, anything to defend himself with, but the drawer in the nightstand only contained a Bible. Adrenaline rushed through his veins and his blood pressure rose as he wished more than anything that he had returned to Uriel's apartment before coming back here to retrieve his--

"This?" Gabriel asked, taking his iron spike from the desk drawer.

He drew in a sharp breath. "Give that to me."

"Oh, sweetie. Now, you know that's not what's up." She tossed it to Cam who caught it, stood, and walked over, lumbering over Cain as he backed himself against the door.

"I want you to know," Cam told him, his voice steady. "I take no pleasure in this. I'm only doing it because I have to."

"*Angels*," Cain fumed. "Always so smug. You may be God's Wrath and you very well may be able to kill me once and for all but to be clear, I won't make it easy." In one fluid motion, he kneed Cam squarely in the testicles, bringing his foot down hard and stomping on his foot. He pushed his way past, retrieving the book from the nightstand, and swinging it around, slamming it into the side of Cam's face.

Cam grunted, wiping the blood from his lip. "Why are you tryin' to aggravate me?"

Cain leaped onto the bed and hopped down on the other side, putting himself directly in front of the other angel.

She flashed him a condescending smile. "I wouldn't."

"But, I must." He rushed behind her, wrapping his arm around her neck. He spotted a pen on the desk and grabbed it, biting the cap off, spitting it out, and holding the point to her throat. "I'll kill her. I'll jam this into her carotid. She'll bleed out so fast, she'll be dead before she has time to heal."

Camael's face contorted in hatred, his skin flushing, sweat beading on his brow.

Gabriel cleared her throat. "Oh, yeah, you done fucked up now."

Cam flew at them, yanking Cain's hand away from his sister's neck, and snapping his wrist. He flung him across the room into the wall as he screamed in pain. Cam's eyes were wild as he stepped closer, like a bull finally out of its cage.

Cain picked up a lamp and smashed it into his face, but the angel was unfazed. He went for the window, but Cam pulled him back, tossing him like a rag doll to the other side of the room. Again, he tried to open the door, and again, it wouldn't budge. He darted back to the nightstand, removing the drawer, and crashing it over Cam's head. Blood trickled down his temple, but he didn't pause for a second. He kept coming like the villain in a slasher film, unflinching as if he had no pain receptors. He was an automaton, built for one thing and one thing only.

He seized Cain's throat, slamming him hard against the door, his breathing that of wild boar, heavy and snarling. He twirled the plow, a low, guttural laugh escaping his lips as the second-generation human struggled to get free. This was it. They both knew it. This was the end.

With an exasperated groan, Camael drove the spike hard into Cain's chest, plunging it through the muscle and bone, and piercing his fast-beating heart. As he removed the weapon, Cain fell, his eyes rolling back, his body going limp.

Cam dropped the plow and backed away, turning to look at his sister, who was already beginning to cry. "Hey," he said, walking toward her as she got down from her spot on the desk. The sight of her in tears flipped his mood like a switch. All of the anger and violent impulses left him. He was himself again. "Don't be upset. You'll see me later."

"Not like this," she wept.

"Listen, I know it doesn't seem fair, everything done to Cain comes back on the perpetrator times seven, but I understand. You know I do. To be honest with you, it's just nice knowing I have a purpose."

She nodded, letting the tears stream down her flushed cheeks.

"You called in the bomb threat? Everyone else is out of here?"

Again, she nodded.

"Good." He patted her cheek and rubbed her arm. "You know what you gotta do, right?"

"I don't want to."

"But you'll do it, anyway?"

"Yeah."

He offered a sympathetic smile. "You know I love you."

"I know. I know that you do." She hugged him, wiping her tears on his sleeve. "I love you, too. I love you so *so* much."

As she pulled away, he laughed, looking down at the wet spot on his arm. "You'll be fine. The others will take care of you. You should open up to Barachiel more. Stop treating him like a child. I know he's got problems, but he'll be there for you. You know that."

"I will agree if you do me a favor."

"Anything."

"When you see Michael, tell him to take care of Lucifer when he gets there. He's been gone a long time and Heaven is, you know, *an adjustment.* And say 'hi' to Raph for me. Tell him I'm sorry I wasn't there to protect him."

"I will, but you know that wasn't your fault."

"Logically," she whimpered. "But most of the time, it feels like *everything* is my fault."

"Gabriel," He put his finger under her chin to lift her head, looking her in the eyes. "You're not God."

"No, I'm not. Can you imagine?"

They both laughed.

"So," he looked back at Cain's corpse. "How long before--" His hand flew to his chest, the sudden pain gripping him tight, like a hot poker searing through his internal organs. He dropped to his knees and toppled over onto his back, his face losing color and his mouth filling with blood.

Gabriel knelt next to him, hands shaking, her tears running down her cheeks, dripping from her face to her brother's chest. Blood spewed from his lips and trickled from his nose as he gasped for air. He trembled all over as Gabriel watched, unable to live with what was happening. "No," she squeaked. "I won't let you go." She placed her hands over his on his chest as light poured from them. She concentrated, shaking as she mustered everything in her to heal him, but nothing changed. He was still dying.

"It's no use," he gurgled. "I'm *supposed* to go. *It's okay.*" His gaze drifted from her to the ceiling, going distant, like he was looking at something she couldn't see. "G," he said, his voice barely above a whisper. "You didn't tell me it was so beautiful." His eyes closed, one last exhale escaping his lungs as his hand slid from his chest to the floor.

Gabriel covered her mouth, muffling her screams as she sobbed, squeezing her eyes shut as the grief swept her up like a hurricane. She couldn't handle this much pain. She was drowning.

After a few moments, she brushed the tears from her face, steadied her breath, and cracked her neck. She stood up, opened the window behind her, and sat on the sill. With a wave of her hand, both bodies erupted in plumes of smoke and Holy Fire. In a flash of light, Camael's true form burst from the flames, shooting up through the ceiling, and disappearing from her view. She blew a kiss in his direction, slung her leg over the window frame, and hopped out onto the sidewalk. She wiped her nose on her sleeve as she shuffled along the pavement. Her eyelids were heavy as she noticed the first hints of sunrise filling the sky with a purplish glow. Her chest felt heavy and her legs were numb. She lumbered her way to Wendy's, it being so much closer than home, barely aware of her surroundings, exhausted and desperate for bed.

Chapter 20

"Normally, we'd kill your progeny first." Hartley shackled Hattie to the post on the roof of the club, careful not to chip her recently manicured nails on the chains. "I don't know why the Queen wants it done this way, but it's not exactly my place to ask, so. Any last words?"

Hattie looked up at her in defiance, the concrete of the roof hot on her cheek and the holes, pouring blood from where her fangs used to be, aching in her gums. "I won't beg for my life."

"Good, I hate that shit."

She spat on her boots.

"Bitch, I just bought these!" She kicked her in the gut and stomped to the door, slamming it behind her, leaving Hattie alone to watch her first sunrise in decades.

She could hear her screams as she took her phone from her back pocket and dialed the Queen, peering through the tinted window in the door. She watched as Hattie cooked, her veins showing brightly through plumping skin. Her eyes popped, blood pouring from every orifice. After a few moments, her entire body exploded, sending bits of flesh, blood, and gore spewing in all directions. "Gross."

"Yes?" Allydia answered.

"It's done. Is there anything else you need before I go to bed?"

"No, Hartley, get some rest," the Queen told her. "You've done well. But when the sun sets again, find the girl."

Allydia set the phone back on the nightstand, plugging its cord in so it could charge while she slept. She looked fondly and then with concern at her lover asleep next to her. She knew he'd be displeased if he knew what she was up to, but what could she do? The last time a vampire sired without her consent and went unpunished, the consequences had been dire, to say the least. Hundreds had died when the fledgling lost control and gorged himself on an entire village before killing his maker. She couldn't let something like that happen again. It was her responsibility. They were *all* her responsibility, which is why from then on, she insisted on personally approving every turning. Right or wrong, the decision to make someone one of them would be hers, ensuring their loyalty and protecting them from one another. So, though she had been fond of Hattie, she had to reprimand her, if only as a warning to the others. Her behavior could *not* be tolerated.

As for the girl, though, she was torn. She was the product of an unsanctioned act and if she was anyone else, she wouldn't hesitate for a second in putting her down. But, the girl had meant something to Wyatt's son and if he found out that she'd killed her, he would never forgive her. She knew it. She knew it in her soul. He would leave her, his inner angel stronger than his feelings for her. If she was being honest with herself, the rebels weren't entirely wrong. Having him in her life *had* made her a little soft. Never before in her existence as a vampire had she concerned herself with the feelings or opinions of a man. She'd found them to be all but useless, unsatisfying, and obnoxious. But, not him. Wyatt was different. She was drawn to him like a moth to a flame, his light so bright, when she looked at him, nothing else could be seen. She put him above everything, dividing her loyalties and clouding her judgement. He made her question her decisions, her behavior, and her priorities. Being with him had changed her and she wasn't sure that she'd ever be her old self again. So, what to do? What should she do with the girl? She slipped off her clothes. She'd have to mull it over and make a decision after she had the girl in custody. For now, she'd focus on making herself, and her lover, happy.

She climbed on top of him and placed him inside her.

He drew in a sharp breath and opened his eyes, looking up at her and putting his hands on her hips. "Morning."

"Did you sleep well?"

"Not as well as I woke up."

She smiled and gripped the headboard as she moved, delighting in the pleasure washing over his face. Yes, having him in her life had made her soft. One could go as far as to say he made her weak. But, he also made her feel things she hadn't in centuries if she ever had at all. He made her feel cared for and appreciated. He made her feel like he wanted her and not just because of the pheromones. He made her feel needed.

As the sun climbed higher in the sky and her body grew tired, she let him take charge, rolling her onto her back and throwing her leg up around his. She bit her bottom lip, drawing a little blood and swallowing it, something she still had to do now and then when the pleasure was too great and she thought she might lose control. She didn't want to hurt him. She never wanted to hurt him.

Chapter 21

Wendy finished packing, picked up her suitcase, and made her way back to the living room where the coven waited to say 'goodbye'. She gave each woman a hug as they left through the patio door.

"If you're ever back our way, give me a call," Alice said. "You can come stay with me. No sense wasting money on a hotel."

"Thank you, Alice. I'll do that."

When the other ladies had gone, Charlotte gave her a quick hug, patting her back and smiling. "I just want to say, thank you so much. You really saved our bacon back there. I don't know what we would have done if you hadn't come."

"It was my pleasure," Wendy told her.

"I hope we didn't pull you away from anything too important."

"More important than this?"

She laughed. "Well, maybe some*one* important? There is someone special isn't there? Don't try to hide it. I have a sense about these things."

"Oh, do you?"

"Hey, you feel magic, I feel love. So?"

She bit her bottom lip. "*Maybe* there's *someone*."

"I knew it. And how do they feel about all this, taking over your grandmother's magical helpline, so to speak?"

"Oh, I haven't told her, yet."

Charlotte cast a judgemental glare her way.

"I said *yet*. She has a lot to deal with right now. Some guy her dad screwed over forever ago is still pissy about it, I guess, so she's got a situation to handle. Plus, I'm not really sure how to bring it up, you know? I've been doing this since I was a teenager. It's why I became a flight attendant, for the free travel to wherever I'm needed. My grandmother taught me, but it's been just me, on my own, for a long time, keeping this secret. I *will* tell her, though."

"All right, well, take my advice, do it sooner rather than later. Secrets are poison to a relationship. Just ask my ex-husband."

They both laughed as the older woman stepped out onto the patio. "And Wendy,"

"Yeah?"

"I only knew your grandmother by reputation, but I think she'd be really proud of you."

She smiled. "I hope so."

Chapter 22

Gabriel stumbled into Wendy's apartment, ignoring the fact that the door was unlocked when she got there. She plopped down on the couch and leaned her head back, annoyed that she'd have to wait a little longer to get some rest. "Sup, Poe?"

"How did you know I was here? How did you know my name?" She let the invisibility spell fall as she looked over the woman sitting next to her.

"I know most things."

"I'm looking for We--"

"She's in New Zealand. I *won't* be telling her you stopped by."

"Oh, are you her, I mean, are you guys like, a thing? Because *we* aren't. I'm Ace. I'm not into her, I swear."

"I'm not worried about that, kid. I haven't known Wendy that long, but I'm pretty sure she's not a pedophile. It's your witch war I don't want her getting dragged into." She stood up and shuffled to a window, opening it, and holding out her hand. "I appreciate you coming to warn her, but she can protect herself. Cute rabbit. Just the right amount of massacre-y." A checkbook flew into her hand from outside. She looked around the room for a pen, finding one on the coffee table next to a stack of mail.

"Is this real?" Poe wondered aloud.

She filled out the check for one million dollars and handed it to the girl. "Cash it. Hide out somewhere. Mostly, just try not to die. Wendy would be upset if something happened to you and if she cries, I'm gonna cry and I am way past my limit of depressing shit. Oh, fuck me. I probably broke a window at my place. Oh, well. Future problems."

"You're a witch, too?"

"No."

"But, how did you--"

"I'm something else. Listen, I'm not trying to be a dick, but I've had a real shitty night and it would be super awesome if you could go somewhere else now."

"Oh. Yeah, sure." She stood up and put her pack on, looking at the check in her hand for the first time. "Holy shit! A million dollars?"

"You're still here."

"I can't take this. You don't even know me."

She sighed, sitting back down. "Poe, real name Angela Hessen, born to a fourteen-year-old rape victim named Jessica Weber who died of an overdose when you were six days old. Adopted seven months later by the Hessens who kicked you out two years ago. After a short stint living on the streets, Grace found you and took you in. She recognized you as a direct descendant of Merga Bein, who, back in sixteen-o-three, used some powerful as shit magic to transfer her pregnancy to another witch before she was burned at the stake. You like tacos and the color purple. Spring is your favorite season and you wear black because you hope it'll make you seem scary or sad enough that people will leave you alone. Now, you're freaking out. You're thinking, 'How does this strange woman know all this?' 'Is she psychic?' 'I never knew my real mom's name before.' Girl, for real. I need to lay down. Please go away."

Poe stared, slack-jawed, and dumbfounded. "What the fuck are you?"

"I'm intuitive. I'm upset. I'm a little fucked up and I'm tired...of *everything*."

Chapter 23

Navid read his newspaper, patiently waiting at the gate of the airport until the sun had come up. Allydia had demanded he go back to London, but he never got on the plane. Instead, he waited, knowing that she and the rest of her kind would soon be fast asleep, allowing him to move freely among them as he investigated. He needed to know more, not only about his family and their past but about vampires. Knowing that they were real and not some comic book myth as he'd always thought was more than a shock; it was mind-blowing. He couldn't get his head around it. Vampires. It was insane. How could it be true? But, he'd seen it. He'd seen the fangs and the strange, dilated pupils with his own eyes. He'd heard the conversation between Allydia and the man that killed his mother. They hadn't known he was there. There was no reason for them to be lying. Moreover, Allydia had seemed sincere in her explanation of things. As a detective, he knew when someone was deceiving him. At least, he liked to think that he did.

Now that he knew her name, he was able to track down an address for his long-lost ancestor. Not many "Allydia Cain's" living in Manhattan, or anywhere else, for that matter. She was the only one, as far as he could tell. She owned property all over the world: apartments in Vancouver, Toronto, Tokyo, Paris, and Madrid. Hotels in Barcelona and Prague. Brothels in Amsterdam. Houses in Athens, Lisbon, and Milan. Medieval castles, now working museums, all over Europe. She owned nightclubs in Hamburg, Seville, Glasgow, Zurich, and Jerusalem. Game preserves in Nairobi and a shopping mall in Rabat. It was an impressive list, but what he was interested in right now were her holdings in the US. He scrolled through the list on his phone. There were nightclubs in Chicago, Los Angeles, New Orleans, and New York. He'd been to the Manhattan nightclub once before but it had been overrun with what he now knew to be vampires. He made a mental note to visit there again before moving on.

Hotels in the French Quarter, on the Vegas Strip, and in Beverly Hills. Casinos in Reno and Atlantic City. And, finally, an apartment building on the Upper West Side. He jotted down the address, set the newspaper on his seat, and left the airport.

"West Eighty-Ninth and Amsterdam," he told the cabbie as he got in the back seat.

"Sure thing," he replied, turning the key and pulling out onto the road. "From out of town?"

"It's that obvious?"

"The accent gives it away."

"Right."

"Seein' any shows while you're here?"

"I've already seen one," he said, the memory of Allydia's teeth flashing in his mind. "Not sure I could handle another."

"Take my advice, kid. See as many as you can. Life is short. You might not get another chance."

Navid made quick work of picking the lock of the penthouse door, slipping inside undetected. He poked his head into every room, seeing that they were empty before moving on to the next. He peeked in drawers, went through closets and kitchen cabinets. He didn't know what he was looking for; he just needed to know more.

He opened the fridge and covered his mouth with the back of his hand. Inside were several bottles of wine, a bottle of rum, and blood bags. The bags hung from metal bars affixed to the ceiling of the appliance in four rows. Upon closer inspection, he could see that they were organized by blood type and expiration date. There was no food anywhere in the kitchen. This was it. This was what she lived on. He closed the fridge and wandered to the living room, noticing a door he hadn't seen in his initial walk-through. Behind it was a flight of stairs which he took to the roof, the scent of gardenias flooding his sinuses. They grew in large bushes in raised beds, the only plants in the rooftop garden. He picked one, brought it to his nose, and breathed in its sweet and refreshing fragrance.

He went downstairs, taking one last look around the apartment before deciding there was nothing of interest there. Now that he wasn't focused on his investigation, he could appreciate how beautiful the apartment was. There were antique chaises, ornate rugs, and gorgeous stenciling on the walls of the living room and bedrooms. The rich, hardwood floors flowed throughout and deep purple curtains covered every window. Allydia had excellent taste, if not a little over the top.

As he made his way to the front door to leave, he realized he was still carrying the flower he'd taken from the roof. Not wanting to leave any evidence of his presence, he shoved it in his pocket before exiting, making sure to lock up on his way out.

Navid broke into the nightclub with the same level of ease he had the apartment. It was dark, the main level having no windows, the dim lights just bright enough that he could make out the shapes of tables and booths around the walls. The room was mostly empty, serving as a dance floor most nights. Aside from the main entrance, there were two fire exits on either side of the room, their signs shining red above them. He swept the room, looking under tables and behind light fixtures, for what, he didn't know. This was his training, to go over everything, leaving no stone unturned. The place was spotless. Not a hint of the debauchery that must have gone on there at night between the creatures that haunted it.

He turned his eyes to the upper level and crept up the staircase. There, he found a VIP area, roped off, and a door. He ignored the booth, the door drawing him to it somehow. To his surprise, it was unlocked, so he went inside, his eyes widening at the sight of the room. There were beautiful paintings and tapestries hanging from the walls, settees, small tables, and a rug he recognized as being ancient

Mesopotamian. He wasn't sure if it was Babylonian or Assyrian, but he knew it was old and probably priceless. He was still marveling at how perfectly preserved it seemed when his gaze lifted to the throne. Huge and ornately carved, the throne with its plush, mulberry seat loomed, as if it would come to life and swallow him whole at any moment.

He jumped, startled by what sounded like a doorknob turning. He turned to see a beautiful woman exiting what looked to be a bedroom.

"I'm sorry, my Queen," she blurted, rubbing the sleep from her eyes. "The sun was out and I didn't want to risk--" She stopped, confusion replacing panic in her expression. She rushed toward him, pinning him to the wall as she breathed in his scent. "I thought you were the Queen. You smell like the Queen. *What have you done with the Queen?*"

"Nothing," he stammered, remembering the flower in his pocket. He pulled it out and showed it to her. "It's just the gardenia. I took it from her garden. That's all."

"You steal from Her Majesty, break in here, and have the audacity to say, 'that's all'?"

"I'm sorry. I just wanted to learn more about her. I'd never lay a hand to hurt her, I swear it."

She smelled him again, almost touching her nose to his throat as he struggled to get free. "The gardenia, yes. But not just that. There's something else. Something in the blood. Who are you?"

He squirmed against her hand, but it was useless. She had him. "I don't think she'd want me telling you, miss."

She lowered her head and looked up at him, allowing her eyes to go black.

"All right, all right. I get it. You're creepy. But I could ask you the same question, mm? These are obviously her rooms. Who are you to be here when she's not?"

She stared, her face tight as she defended herself. "I am Hartley Morales, assistant to the Queen. I'm here because finishing work for Her Majesty left me stranded. Walking home in the daylight isn't exactly an option for me." She slid her hand up from his chest to his neck, applying a small amount of pressure without inhibiting his breathing. "Your turn."

His heart beat faster as he considered his options. Telling her who he was could be painting a giant target on his back. On the other hand, she was one snarky comment away from snapping his neck like a dry twig. He tried to think of a lie, but nothing he came up with would have made sense. As the adrenaline flooded his brain, he decided the best course of action was to spit it out and hope for the best.

"Fine. *Fine.* My name is Navid Parsi. I discovered Allydia stalking me back in London, so I followed her here. She told me I'm her descendant through my mother's line. I just wanted to find out more about her and where I come from. She told me it wouldn't be safe for me here. Told me to go home. Probably should've listened."

Hartley's face went pale, her eyes like saucers as she yanked her hand away. "Her trip," she realized. "A living relative. I can't believe it. Here I was thinking low-key Thor was her greatest weakness. At least *he* can take care of himself. You, you're helpless. If the rebels find out about *you*," She grabbed his collar. "You have to go."

She dragged him out of the room, past the VIP area, and down the stairs, texting as she went. "You shouldn't have come here," she lectured. "It's day, so it's probably all right, but I'm sending a human security guard to look out for you until you get on a plane, just in case."

"That's hardly necessary," he told her as she let him go at the bottom of the steps.

She smacked her lips. "Maybe, but I'm not risking the hellfire she'll reign down on me if something happens to you because I didn't take precautions. A *human*." She gave him a quick once over. "That's heavy." She took his arm and pulled him toward the exit.

"I'm a detective. I don't need a bodyguard."

"Um, yeah, you do. Don't worry about it. You won't even know he's there. Just get your ass home with a quickness." She opened the door and pushed him out, staying behind it to avoid the sun's rays.

Thrust out onto the sidewalk, he breathed a sigh of relief, the door slamming shut in front of him. "Well, that could have gone worse." He put his hand out to hail a cab as he thanked his lucky stars that nothing terrible had happened. Soon, one stopped and he got in. "JFK, please, mate."

The driver nodded and pulled away as Navid took one last look at the club, his hopes of getting to know more about his lineage dwindling as the building faded from view.

Chapter 24

"Stop right here, mate," Navid told the driver as he drove past the bakery, the light from its sign casting a glow on the dark street. The owner sat on the pavement outside, head in hands, openly weeping as police bustled around in the building.

"What's happened?" he asked, hurrying from the cab to his friend. He placed a hand on the man's shoulder and peeked inside. The place was trashed. Tables were flipped, chairs were broken, and smashed glass was everywhere. "Shit. They've come back?"

Babak nodded.

"I'm so sorry. I thought they'd gone for good 'round here. These ABM boys will never learn, will they? Don't you worry, though. I'll find the ones that done this. I swear, I'll--"

"It doesn't matter anymore, Navid. Nothing matters."

"What do you mean? They've got to pay for what they've done and I'll make sure they do, yeah? In the meantime, I'll help you clean up, get things settled."

"No. No, I won't be reopening. I'm done. I'm going home."

"Home? You mean to Tehran?"

"Yes."

"But, what about--"

"They killed her, Navid," he said, his voice booming in the night air. "They murdered my Shadi."

His mouth fell open as he dropped down to sit next to his friend.

"I was at the market. We were running low on eggs. I was only gone for fifteen minutes, maybe twenty. When I came back, I found her in the mess, blood all over. There was so much blood, I couldn't tell where it was coming from. Her whole body was soaked." He covered his mouth and sobbed.

Navid put his arm around him and fought back tears of his own. "I'm so sorry, my friend. I'm so, so sorry."

"I will take her home to be buried in Zahara's Paradise. I will demand the body washers be gentle. It is the least I can do. It is what she would want."

"Of course. Of course, take her home. Is there anything I can do for you? Anything at all?"

He shook his head.

"All right, how about I just sit with you then? I'll sit right here until you tell me you don't need me anymore, yeah?"

"Thank you. You're a good boy, Navid. One day, if you're lucky, you will find *your* Shadi. Someone to make you happy, feed you pastries until you get fat like me."

"I don't know about that. But, yeah, maybe if I'm really lucky." The two sat there in the dark, allowing the silence to wash over them as they mourned.

As soon as he opened the door to his flat, he wished he hadn't. Before he stepped foot inside, a hand flew out and jerked him in. It belonged to a large man, maybe six foot five, with long, unwashed, black hair. The door slammed behind him. He turned to see another man, shorter with blond hair and eyes so green, they looked like they'd been colored in with a marker. The big man tossed him onto the sofa and stood over him as the other sat down, draping his arm over the back of the couch and sucking on his teeth.

"Who might you be, then?" the blond man asked.

"I was about to ask that of you. Who are you? What do you want?"

"We ask the questions, bruv."

"This is my place, right? So, I'll be askin' whatever questions I like."

"Ah, is that right?"

'Yeah, mate. That's right."

"Do you hear that, Simon? He'll ask whatever he likes."

The big man snorted.

"Well, in that case, I'm Jack. This is my associate, Simon. We're here on King's business. See, he knows that that harpy that calls herself Queen was following you about, but what he can't figure is what for. He's stumped. But, I bet you know, don't ya?"

"King? What are you on about? What King?"

"Wrong answer, Nav." He socked him in the gut so hard, he thought he might throw up. The wind was knocked out of him and it took him a minute to catch his breath. "The King of our people is who I'm speakin' of, Nav. The true King. Now, sure, he's not the first of our kind or nothin', but he understands us. He's one of us, you get me? Unlike that bitch in her ivory tower, forcing us to fight for humans, takin' up with a lightning wizard, our King is for *us*. He's lookin' to unseat the harpy permanently, you understand? And he needs leverage. You, Navid Parsi, are that leverage. Only question is, how important are you to Her Majesty? What are you, eh? Boy toy? Blood bag? Inside man in law enforcement? What's so special about you that the old bag felt the need to creep around here like a virgin outside a whorehouse?"

"He's too pretty to be smart," Simon chimed in. "Probably not much of a detective. I'm guessing side piece."

"Is that it, Nav? Is the old bint letting you get your end away? Or has it not gotten that far? Rumor has it before she started shaggin' the American, she followed him 'round like a cat in heat, too. A desperate puppy, she was. Is that what's going on here? The Queen fancies ya?"

"That is absolutely not what's going on."

"What then? Come on, give us the dish."

He clenched his jaw.

"Oh, you won't tell me?"

"Sorry, boys. I'm not feeling particularly chatty."

"That's very disappointing, Nav. See, the King wants this information. Without it, he doesn't know if he should take you prisoner, or kill you offhand."

"I say we kill him," Simon grunted.

"Now, Simon, you know it's not our place to make those decisions."

"What is your place, Jack?" Navid sassed. "On your knees in front of some bloke calling himself your King?"

Jack slapped him, whipping his head to the side and causing his lip to bleed. "That was a warning, Nav. It'll be a lot easier on ya if you cooperate."

"Yeah," Simon smirked. "I'd hate to do you like your friend at the bakery."

He glared up at him, his cheeks burning. "What did you say?"

"The old lady. When you weren't here, we tried the bakery. No one there but her. We got a little frustrated, so we decided to have a laugh."

Navid's common sense left him as his heart pounded in his ears, fury burning through him like wildfire. He kicked his foot out hard, breaking Simon's shin before headbutting him in the chest, knocking him to the ground. He jumped up from his seat and turned to punch Jack squarely in the nose. While they were stunned, he made a beeline for the door. But, the vampires were fast, pulling him back and throwing him to the floor. Knowing there wasn't a minute to spare, he swept his leg, knocking Simon down. He landed with a thud as Navid got to his feet, dodging Jack's right hook. He avoided another hit and another, backing from the living room toward the kitchen. He feigned reaching for something on the bar with his left hand, distracting Jack just long enough to land a jab with his right.

"Oh, you'll pay for that, Nav," Jack warned, rubbing his jaw. In a blur, Jack was on him, pushing him to the floor and pounding his face and stomach with his pale, freckled fists.

"I wanna play," Simon said, hurrying over. He kicked him in the side over and over, crowing as he felt his ribs crack through his shoe.

"Hold on, hold on," Jack said, waving his hand at Simon. "Do you smell that?"

"Yeah," Simon gleaned. "Blood."

"No, somethin' else. Somethin' in it. You smell that?" They got down on the floor, sniffing Navid's wounds. "Could it be?" Jack licked the blood from a gash on Navid's cheek as he fought to keep conscious. "Well, I'll be goddamned."

"What is it?"

"It's her. It's the bloody Queen. This poor sod is one of hers. Blood of her blood."

"Aren't we all blood of her blood?"

"Yeah, technically, but this one's *human*. Don't ya get it?"

Simon stared blankly.

Jack rolled his eyes. "Come on, you can't be this dense. He's a human descendant of the Queen."

"He's a *what*?"

"Exactly! That's why she was so interested in seein' what he was up to. The old cow was pinin' for her real family."

"I didn't know she had any."

"Well, me, neither. I don't think anyone did. The King certainly hasn't the foggiest. You know what this means, don't ya?"

"What?"

"We bring him in, *alive*, we'll be heroes. The King will give us riches beyond our wildest dreams. Maybe Governorships, even."

"Alive?" His eyes went black. "I see what you're sayin' but that's a lot of blood going to waste."

"We'll pick up some skags once we've got him secure on the plane, right? He's our golden ticket, Simon. Best we don't fuck it up, yeah?"

"I guess."

"Good. Get the trunk ready. Let's see how flexible our boy here is." Simon went to the hall closet and dragged out a large steamer trunk. He opened it up, glancing inside to make sure there were enough air holes poked into the sides. Jack smiled down at Navid who lay half-unconscious and unable to move. "Come on, bruv. Don't want to keep His Majesty waiting."

Chapter 25

Lucifer's cold body lay draped on his bed, stale blood staining the sheets under his still-open mouth. It was empty, his true form having vacated hours before, on to another adventure.

His footsteps echoed in the suffocating silence of the sprawling nothing that was Purgatory. He trudged through the cold and dark, the hollowness of it more unsettling than the most depraved sewers of Hell. Above him, the souls hung, all of them unaware of the others just next to them, quiet and contemplative. It was a ghastly sight, even for Lucifer.

He trekked on, undeterred. Finally, he came upon the soul he'd been searching for. The figure of light hovered in front of him, still, content in its misery. He stood before it, watching with glee as the image of a face began to take form on what appeared to be its hanging head. Its glowing eyes looked up at him, warning him to leave it be. His eyes twinkled in the shimmer of the soul's incandescence and a sly smile crept across his face. "Hello, nephew."

The End

The Complete Seventh Day Series

Seraphim
Nephilim
Elohim
Cain
Alukah
Coven
Sinclair

Printed in Great Britain
by Amazon